Without a Trace

Eight-year-old Maisie Brown disappeared during Tanniford's annual fête. Chief Inspector Millson suspected Maisie's stepfather. Millson disliked stepfathers. His own daughter had one and he resented having to arrange with him and his ex-wife when he could see her.

Tanniford lay in the bend of a river, confined there by the railway line. The only road out was over the railway bridge. The local police had closed the road to traffic while the fête was on and no vehicle left the village between two o'clock and six that day. This convinced Millson that Maisie had been abducted by someone in the village and she was still there—dead or alive. The villagers believed a stranger had taken her. In a way, they were both right.

MALCOLM FORSYTHE

Without a Trace

THE CRIME CLUB
An Imprint of HarperCollins *Publishers*

First published in Great Britain in 1991
by The Crime Club, an imprint of
HarperCollins Publishers, 77–85 Fulham Palace Road,
Hammersmith, London W6 8JB

9 8 7 6 5 4 3 2 1

First published 1991

British Library Cataloguing in Publication Data

A catalogue record for this book is
available from the British Library

ISBN 0 00 232370 2

Photoset in Linotron Baskerville by
Rowland Phototypesetting Ltd
Bury St Edmunds, Suffolk
Printed and bound in Great Britain by
HarperCollins Book Manufacturing, Glasgow

SATURDAY

CHAPTER 1

Eight-year-old Maisie Brown, blonde, blue-eyed drum majorette, was kidnapped on the day of Tanniford's annual fête. She disappeared like a card from a magician's hand. One moment she was there, talking to her friend Vicki Calcot, the next moment she'd vanished.

The Tanniford Regatta and Fête took place every year on the second or third Saturday in July, depending upon which day the river was at low tide in the afternoon. At low tide, the small cargo vessels that unloaded at the timber port were unable to navigate the narrow river and the villagers were allowed to rope the river off above and below the village and hold their regatta.

Tanniford lay in a bend of the river. A railway line running alongside the river continued in a straight line across the bend, confining the village between it and the river. There was no bridge over the river and the only way into and out of Tanniford was by the bridge across the railway cutting at the top of the High Street. It was a restriction Ted Baxter, the local policeman, made use of on fête day by erecting a barrier on the bridge to prevent traffic entering or leaving the village. He was able to say later that no vehicle entered or left the village between two o'clock and six that Saturday.

The day of the fête was warm and sunny and visitors flocked into Tanniford from miles around. Cars and other vehicles were diverted to a car park in a field above the village where the Tanniford Scout Troop directed the drivers into roped-off lanes and helped them to park neatly.

At half past two a mini-coach arrived in the car park, delivering ten of Madame Hawksby's drum majorettes. The mini-coach was followed by a small red hatchback from which Madame Hawksby herself emerged, heaving herself with difficulty from the driving seat. Edith Hawksby had once been a dancer with a figure like a sylph—but that had been a long time ago.

The ten majorettes were joined by four from Tanniford waiting in the car park, who included Maisie Brown and her friend Vicki Calcot. The fourteen girls were aged between seven and sixteen and identically dressed in scarlet dress and cape, long white gloves and white ankle boots. From hat-boxes in the mini-coach, Madame Hawksby handed out the tall toy-soldier hats covered with gold braid that completed the outfit.

'Fall in!' Madame Hawksby barked the command like a sergeant-major.

The girls crammed the hats down on their heads so they wouldn't fall off when they were marching and formed up in three lines. Madame Hawksby walked slowly along the lines inspecting each girl in turn. She made corrections—a hat not the right angle here, a cape crooked there. She examined their faces, checking make-up. Madame Hawksby insisted upon make-up for even the youngest of her girls and they all had rosy cheeks, red lips and sparkling eyes. Not a pale face among them. The make-up was not so much to add glamour to their appearance as to achieve the uniformity that was an essential element of the performance.

When she was satisfied all was well, Madame Hawksby waddled to the front and delivered her usual exhortations.

'Remember . . . backs straight, bottoms in. And *smile*! Smile all the time. Show your teeth. And get those knees up *high*!'

On the road outside the car park, the procession of floats and exhibits had already lined up. At the front of the parade was the regimental band from Colchester barracks and bringing up the rear, on the last float, was the carnival queen and her entourage from Walton-on-the-Naze.

Madame Hawksby's girls, led by the tallest—sixteen-year-old Zena Baz—trooped out of the car park and took up their positions at the head of the parade in front of the band.

Zena raised her three-foot baton high in the air. A big drum began beating. The girls picked up the step and the band struck up a martial tune. Zena brought the baton down smartly and, watched by an admiring crowd, fourteen high-stepping majorettes set off across the railway bridge and down the High Street lined with spectators.

The majorettes led the parade down the High Street, past the shops on the right and the Falcon pub and churchyard on the left and turned right into West Street. At the railway station they would turn up Station Road to rejoin the High Street at the bridge and continue into Ferry Street opposite, on a route that circled the village and led eventually back to the square at the bottom end of the High Street.

The Reverend Vernon Smollett emerged from his vicarage behind the Falcon and entered the churchyard packed with stalls and sideshows. He was delighted to see a long queue at the church door. People were queuing to pay the fee for taking a rubbing from the brasses in the chancel over the burial sites of John de Vere and his wife Elizabeth. The money would go into the restoration fund for the church tower. The Vicar particularly wanted to repair the rickety wooden stairway at the top of the tower. The stairway gave access to the roof from where there was a wonderful view over the whole of Tanniford.

The Vicar made his way through the crowd, nodding to people and exchanging words with the stallholders. One of them was Maisie Brown's mother, Carol, at a Home-made Cakes stall.

'Did you make all these cakes yourself, Mrs Brown?'

'Yes, every one, Vicar.'

'Wonderful . . . wonderful.' He moved on, smiling.

The smile faded into a frown at the sight of young Trudy Wilson behind her father's Home-made Wine stall. Trudy had entered for the Pram Race with her boyfriend, Wayne Green, and she was dressed as a baby girl. A straw bonnet enclosed her golden curls and she wore a short white dress and frilly petticoats that barely covered her lace-trimmed panties as she bent over, applying make-up to Wayne's face.

The Vicar disapproved of the Pram Race. Its main purpose, it seemed to him, was to provide a peepshow and an excuse for a lot of drinking. The men, dressed up as nannies and pushing their 'babies' in an old pram, made a circuit of the pubs in Tanniford, racing from pub to pub and downing a pint of beer at each. By the time they reached the finishing line on the quay—which not all of them did—they were thoroughly drunk.

Once, there had been twenty-pubs in the village. Now there were only six and there wouldn't have been that many, but for the trade from the shipyard and the timber port.

The timber port was comparatively recent but there had been shipbuilding at Tanniford of one sort or another since 1570, before the Spanish Armada. In the Second World War the yard built MTBs for the Royal Navy. Today, the small privately owned shipyard turned out coasting vessels.

Visitors who came to see Tanniford's Norman church or the pargetting on Garrison House were surprised when they wandered along the riverfront and came across a shipyard. It was hidden at the end of the quay, behind a tall building clad with sheets of corrugated iron. There, in a field that had been concreted over, would be the skeleton of a ship under construction and around it, cutters and welders assembling further sections to be lifted into position by an overhead crane.

As Trudy uncapped a lipstick and bent over Wayne again, the Vicar averted his eyes from her eye-dazzling display and moved on.

'Hold still and pout your lips,' Trudy told Wayne.

He made a face at her, his mouth opening in a grin. 'Don't do that!' she said crossly. 'Else I can't put it on properly.'

Trudy had no expectation of winning the Pram Race. Wayne was no great drinker and nor was he a fast runner. It was the other prize she was after, the one for the best-dressed nanny and baby, and she was determined to win it.

She had made the outfit she was wearing. Wayne had been squeezed into a nurse's uniform and a pair of black tights she'd borrowed from a friend. His blonde wig had been hired from Beryl's Hair Salon and the lace cap tied beneath his chin had belonged to her grandmother.

The procession reached the square at the bottom of the High Street on its return journey and halted. The band and the majorettes continued down Anchor Hill on to the quay. The band peeled off to one side in front of the Anchor pub and the majorettes began their display of marching and counter-marching.

It was a popular event and one of the highspots of the afternoon. Everywhere cameras clicked and whirred, photographing flashing limbs and swirling skirts as the girls energetically high-stepped and about-turned up and down the quay.

Among the watching crowd, Ernie Turner's eyes were upon little Maisie Brown. He knew all four Tanniford girls taking part, but eight-year-old Maisie Brown with the blonde hair and blue eyes was his favourite. A real little charmer. She looked doubly attractive today, he thought, catching her eye.

Following Madame Hawksby's instructions, Maisie smiled back at Mr Turner and high-stepped for all she was worth, making the skirt of her dress bounce up and down as she marched.

Maisie liked Mr Turner. Mr Turner was a nice old man who gave her sweets when she went to see him. He was very unhappy because his wife was ill in hospital. Sometimes he sat Maisie on his lap and cuddled her and read stories. She wished Mr Turner was her daddy. In fact, she wished almost anyone was her daddy except Ronald Craig. She didn't like Ronald, but she had to have him because he lived with her mum and her real dad was dead.

At the other end of the quay, Sidney Nunn dropped to one knee and pointed his video camera at Maisie and Vicki Calcot as they came towards him, skirts flaring as they about-turned. He rose to his feet again to film the leader of the troupe, dark-haired Zena Baz. Her breasts were straining the satin bodice of her dress and her upper lip was moist with perspiration. He brought her into focus and operated the zoom lens for a close-up.

Charles Cresswell, standing behind Nunn, watched him with an amused smile. Sixteen-year-old Zena was the daughter of the landlord of the Anchor. She would be leaving school in the autumn and Cresswell, who owned Cresswell Marine further along the quay, had agreed to take her on as a clerk in his office.

The display ended. The procession re-formed in the square and returned up the High Street and over the bridge to its starting point by the car park. There it halted and dispersed.

The majorettes tripped across the car park to where Madame Hawksby was waiting by her car. She'd watched their performance from the balcony of the Anchor with a large gin and tonic in her hand.

'That was very good,' she boomed. 'Well done, girls.'

She collected the hats and returned them to their hat-boxes in the mini-coach. Then she put aboard the ten girls who'd come by road and turned to the four Tanniford girls.

'See you go straight home and change out of your uniforms.'

'Yes, Madame Hawksby,' they chorused.

She climbed into her car and they waved goodbye to her as she drove away.

It was ten minutes to four.

The time for the Pram Race was approaching and all over the village men were appearing dressed as nannies and wheeling old-fashioned prams.

The four Tanniford majorettes left the car park and walked back across the bridge. Two of the girls turned into Station Road. Maisie and her friend, Vicki, continued down the High Street.

Among the spectators spilling into the street after the procession had passed was one of the men dressed as a nanny. His grey wig was cramped into a black bonnet and beneath a long cape he wore a navy-blue skirt. He was wheeling a large black pram and looked much the same way as the other men taking part in the Pram Race.

His eyes followed Maisie Brown and her friend as they walked along the High Street, their scarlet dresses highly visible in the crowd.

The girls stopped outside Nunn's sweetshop and newsagent's. They seemed to be arguing. Then Vicki shrugged her shoulders and went into the shop. Maisie walked on and turned into the narrow alleyway between the butcher's shop and the baker's that led to her home. It was called Blood Alley because it had once been the path to the old abattoir behind the butcher's.

The man dressed as a nanny moved swiftly across the High Street with his pram and turned into Station Road. Behind the estate agent's on the corner he paused briefly to make sure he was unobserved, then plunged into Baker's

Passage. Baker's Passage ran behind the shops in the High Street all the way down to West Street at the bottom. Half way down it crossed Blood Alley.

The man reached the intersection of the two alleyways and stood, breathless and waiting, in Baker's Passage. The junction with Blood Alley was flanked by high brick walls and the windowless wall of the old abattoir.

As she sauntered past the mouth of Baker's Passage, Maisie Brown had a brief glimpse of the gaping neck of a large black bag in the air above her. Then it descended over her head . . . her shoulders . . . and on down to her feet, enveloping her completely.

She began screaming.

Down on the quay, the annual Tug of War across the river between Tanniford's firemen and the shipyard workers ended. The firemen lost and were pulled down the muddy bank into the water. The result of the contest was given out over the public address system, followed by an announcement that the next event would be the Pram Race.

In the churchyard, Trudy Wilson and Wayne Green wheeled their pram out from behind the stall and made their way through the crowd to the gates and into the High Street.

In Blood Alley, the man finished tying the neck of the bag round Maisie's ankles and looped a cord tight around the middle of the bag to pin her arms. Turning her over face down, he folded her legs up behind her and tied her ankles back to the cord round her middle.

He stood up, lifted the mattress and blankets from the pram and took out the bottom boards. Picking up his neatly-trussed captive, he laid her in the bottom of the pram, making sure the brass eyelets inserted into the bag to provide air were unobstructed. He listened for a moment. The sounds within the bag were barely audible. Satisfied, he tossed the bottom boards back in the pram and covered Maisie with the mattress and blankets.

Then, raising the hood, he wheeled the laden pram along Baker's Passage to West Street, stepped boldly out into the street and mingled with the crowd.

It was three minutes past four.

Over the address system came the final call for competitors in the Pram Race to assemble at the starting point on the quay outside the Anchor pub.

Charles Cresswell, whose company had contributed handsomely to the fête in both cash and facilities, was umpiring the event. When the contestants were lined up, he emerged from the committee room in the Anchor to inspect them. There were rules to be complied with.

'Babies' had to be female and over sixteen. Once a man had entered with his five-year-old son and won the race easily. 'Nannies' had to wear full-length skirts to hamper their running. Trousers or mini-skirts were not allowed. And prams had to be original and four-wheeled.

This last rule tended to limit the number of competitors. Genuine perambulators were antiques and hard to come by. The ones in Tanniford were carefully preserved year after year for this event.

Moving along the pairs of competitors, Cresswell came to Trudy and Wayne. Trudy was sucking a dummy and holding a baby's rattle. Cresswell, grey-haired and middle aged, looked her up and down appreciatively and winked.

Randy old goat! Trudy thought.

However, Charles Cresswell would be judging the best-dressed nanny and baby competition later. She gave him a coy smile and fluttered her eyelashes.

'Charming, my dear, charming,' he murmured.

The inspection over, Cresswell blew a whistle for attention. 'Put the babies in the prams!' he shouted.

Wayne lifted up Trudy in a flurry of white frills and laid

her in the pram. It was a small utility pram manufactured after the Second World War and when Trudy wedged herself into the narrow body, her legs dangled over the sides.

'You're showing Monday's washing!' a woman cackled.

As Trudy tried to prise herself up and change her position Cresswell's whistle peeped again and Wayne pushed her back in. At that instant a press photographer stepped forward and took her picture.

'You all know the rules,' Cresswell said. 'Nanny has a pint at every pub—the first one is here.' He pointed to the pints of beer lined up on a table outside the Anchor's bay window. 'Glasses must be completely drained . . . no spilling beer on the ground. The course is the usual one. The Black Dog, Spreadeagle, Falcon, Station Arms, Greyhound . . . in that order. Then back to the Anchor. First couple up to the counter are the winners.'

He put the whistle to his lips. 'All ready?'

He blew the whistle and twelve muscular nannies charged towards the beer-laden table.

At six o'clock that evening Maisie Brown's mother phoned the police and reported her missing.

At six-thirty, after Ted Baxter had lifted the barrier on the bridge, Sidney Nunn's white van drove out of Tanniford.

Before then, at half past five, Carol Brown had called on her sister, Kathy Benson. Kathy was sitting at her desk in the estate agent's on the corner of Station Road and the High Street when the door opened and Carol came in.

There was only a year between them—Kathy was twenty-eight, Carol twenty-seven—but they were very different. Kathy was tall, auburn-haired and calm, like their father. Carol, petite, blonde and excitable, took after their mother.

Kathy looked at Carol in surprise. Although Carol was her sister, she might have been a stranger for all the contact there was between them. Two years it had been. Two years since Carol's husband, Alec, had drowned. And Carol still blamed Kathy for his death.

'Has Maisie been in?' Carol's face was red and perspiring as though she'd been running.

'No, why?'

'Are you sure? I know she comes to see you sometimes.' Carol's tone was accusing. Her eyes darted around wildly, as though the child might be hiding.

'Carol, calm down. She's not here. What's happened?'

'She didn't come home after the parade this afternoon and I can't find her anywhere.'

Kathy's voice was soothing. 'Well, I expect she's with one of her friends. Have you—?'

'Vicki says Maisie was on her way home when she left her outside the sweetshop. That was over an hour ago. Maisie was going home to change and then call for Vicki and they were going round the stalls together. She didn't show up. Vicki thought she'd changed her mind.' Carol's voice rose hysterically. 'Maisie never went home! Her uniform isn't there and the back door key's still on its hook.'

Kathy forced herself to say, 'What about Ronald? Has he seen her?'

Ronald Craig was Maisie's stepfather, though Kathy was reluctant to acknowledge him as that. Carol had taken up with him less than a year after Alec's death and it had deepened the estrangement between Kathy and her sister.

Carol shook her head. 'I've been round everywhere and everyone I can think of. No one has seen her.' She sank into a chair and burst into tears. 'I don't know what to do, Kathy.'

Kathy felt a surge of sympathy. Carol was a worried, bewildered child and Kathy saw her as she used to be . . .

her kid sister in trouble and asking for help. She closed the file she'd been working on and stood up.

'Come on, Sis, we'll look for Maisie together. She must be somewhere you haven't tried. Don't worry, we'll find her.'

She turned the sign on the door to 'Closed' and they went out into the High Street. The fête had ended and visitors were drifting away up the High Street towards the car park.

That evening the local policeman, Ted Baxter, organized a search by the villagers. Gardens, dustbins, sheds . . . the shipyard—all the places a child could be trapped or a child's body concealed.

By nightfall everywhere had been covered. There was no sign of Maisie Brown.

Later, in the dark, Kathy Benson continued searching alone. She was driven by the need to be doing something—anything—rather than sit like Carol, distraught and helpless, awaiting the CID from county headquarters.

If Maisie had fallen in the river and drowned, the shipyard foreman said she'd most likely be washed up on Osea Flats on the outgoing tide during the night.

'Or maybe on the bank by Alresford Creek,' he'd added. 'No good looking in the dark. We'll take a launch downriver at first light.'

The thought of Maisie's drowned body left lying in the mud all night was more than Kathy could bear and she'd followed the riverbank towards Alresford Creek, shining her torch along the water's edge.

Half a mile from Tanniford, as she swept her torch from side to side, the light caught a flash of scarlet—the scarlet of Maisie's dress. With a sob, Kathy started forward. But it was only the remnants of a dinghy spinnaker washed up on the mud.

She reached Alresford Creek and the jagged skeleton of

the old railway bridge that had once spanned it. She could go no further. She turned to retrace her steps, then stopped and listened. Was it her imagination or had she heard something? She strained her ears. There was a sound in the undergrowth further along the creek, a dragging sound. She ran towards it, shining the torch. The noise stopped. Kathy halted and stood listening in the darkness.

Suddenly an arm was flung round her neck from behind. She dropped the torch and clawed frantically at the arm as it tightened relentlessly against her throat, choking her. There was a roaring noise inside her head and then she fainted.

She came to, lying on the ground. Downriver, the sound of an outboard motor receded into the distance.

SUNDAY

CHAPTER 2

Early on Sunday morning, in the small front room of Maisie Brown's home in Bath Street, Detective Chief Inspector George Millson asked her mother a number of routine questions before setting the official police search in operation.

He arrived with Detective-Sergeant Scobie, soon after the Vicar left. The Reverend Vernon Smollett had called to comfort Carol Brown and to let her know the congregation at morning service would pray for Maisie's safe return.

Millson, wearing a grey, chalk-striped suit that fitted him badly, sat in a tub armchair, his bulky figure overflowing it and his long arms hanging over the sides like a gorilla's. Carol Brown thought he looked more like a criminal than a police officer, with his dark hair cropped short and a blue shadow around the lower half of his face as though he hadn't shaved lately. His sandy-haired sergeant was a complete contrast. He was slim, he wore a neat, navy blue suit and he looked thoroughly respectable as he sat on a chair by the window taking notes.

Scobie was twenty-eight, ten years younger than the Chief Inspector. He'd joined George Millson a year ago on transfer from the Met. Millson had been an inspector then and in the Met. Scobie was accustomed to calling his inspector, 'guv'nor'.

'Don't ever call me guv'nor!' Millson had bellowed on their first day together. 'Schools and prisons have governors. I'm an *inspector*.'

'Yes, sir,' said Scobie smartly.

'And you can keep the "sir" for when there's brass about. My name's George. Savvy?'

'Yes. You George, me Norris,' Scobie said good-humouredly.

Millson's thick black eyebrows came together in a frown. '*Norris?* What sort of a name is that?'

'It's Anglo-French. It means "northern". My grandmother was French.'

'I'd keep quiet about that if I were you,' said Millson.

After a year of working together, Scobie had come to admire and respect George Millson. He couldn't decide whether or not he actually liked him, though, and as yet he seldom used his first name.

Carol Brown sat on the sofa, her sister beside her. Kathy had returned to her flat above the estate agent's after the attack last night. Later, she'd come to Carol's house and spent the night trying to comfort her. Kathy hadn't mentioned the attack to Carol, not wanting to upset her further. On the other side of Carol sat Maisie's stepfather, Ronald Craig.

Millson listened to Carol Brown's account of Maisie's disappearance. Then, patiently, he coaxed the answers he needed from her and Scobie wrote them down. Had Maisie ever gone missing before? No, of course not, she told him. Were there any relatives or friends she might have gone to that Carol hadn't checked? No, none. Did she always use that route home from the High Street? Yes. Would she be likely to go off with a stranger? Definitely not. Which men did she know in the village? Practically all of them. Was there one who took a particular interest in her, or was she more friendly with one than with another?

'Not really.' Carol hesitated. 'Well, there's old Ernie Turner, of course. She's often round at his place. His wife's in hospital and Maisie goes round there to cheer him up.'

'Where can we find Mr Turner?'

'He lives in Spring Street—that's just by the Black Dog,'

Carol told him. 'But he won't know anything. I've already asked him.'

Millson nodded non-committally. He intended to question Ernie Turner. In the same way as he would question every man who'd even breathed on the girl. It was routine.

'What was Maisie wearing yesterday?' The search party would have to be briefed on what items of clothing to look for.

Carol stood up and went to the mantelpiece. She picked up a framed photograph of Maisie in her majorette's uniform and handed it to him.

'She was dressed exactly like that—except for the hat.' Her eyes filled with tears.

Millson gazed at the picture of a smiling blue-eyed child in a scarlet drum majorette's outfit. His expression betrayed none of the thoughts going through his mind—that this pretty little blonde girl had probably been abducted and raped. And the odds were she was already dead and he had a murder hunt on his hands. He hoped he was wrong and that this might be the once-in-a-while case a child was recovered safe and well.

'May we borrow this?'

Carol Brown nodded and sat down again. Millson extended one of his long arms and handed the photograph to Scobie, who put it into his briefcase.

'What underclothes was she wearing, Mrs Brown?'

Carol's hand flew to her mouth, her eyes widening in horror.

Kathy put an arm round her shoulders. 'Is that really necessary?'

Millson looked up at her. She was surprised to see compassion in the eyes of this ogre-like man.

'We need to know every item of clothing,' he said gently.

'White cotton knickers . . .' Carol's voice was a whisper.

He nodded. 'Now . . . bear with me. I'd like us to go over

yesterday afternoon again to make sure I have it correctly. Can you do that for me, Carol?'

She looked at him from puffy, tear-filled eyes and nodded.

'After you'd watched Maisie perform in the display on the quay you returned to your Home-Made Cakes stall in the churchyard,' he reminded her. 'And when the parade was over Maisie's friend, Vicki, says they walked down the High Street and parted company outside the sweetshop. Maisie should then have come straight home and changed out of her majorette's uniform. Is that right?'

'Yes.' Carol's voice was shaky. 'She should have been home at four o'clock. I'd left the back door key out for her. When I came in at half-past and she wasn't here I went to her friend's place in East Street, thinking she'd be there. Vicki told me Maisie was on her way home when she last saw her. They'd arranged for Maisie to go over to her house as soon as she'd changed and to walk round the stalls together. That's when I started to panic.'

She broke off with a sob. Kathy patted her hand reassuringly.

Norris Scobie looked up from his notes at Ronald Craig. Maisie's stepfather hadn't comforted Carol once during the interview. A cold fish by the look of him. Craig had a thin, angular body and straight, black hair that flopped over his forehead, making his pale face seem even paler. An indoors man, not a man who saw much sun, Scobie thought.

Carol wiped her eyes with a handkerchief and went on, 'I ran up the High Street and down Blood Alley—the way Maisie would have gone—and back to the house, looking for her. I hoped she'd have come in meantime, but she hadn't. So then I went round every other place I could think of where she might have gone. My sister helped me. No one had seen her.' She put her face in her hands.

Millson nodded sympathetically and turned to Maisie's stepfather. 'And where were you while this was going on, Mr Brown?'

'The name's Craig,' the man said curtly, 'Ronald Craig. We're not married.'

Carol said quickly, 'My husband—Maisie's father—was drowned two years ago. He was a fisherman.'

Millson nodded. He already knew that from Ted Baxter, who'd told him Craig had moved in with Carol Brown a year ago when his wife walked out on him. He looked inquiringly at Craig, awaiting an answer to his question.

'I was helping with a bric-à-brac stall in Station Yard,' Craig said.

'And when did you learn Maisie was missing?'

'Carol told me when I came back to the house about five o'clock.'

'Uh-huh. And just for the record, where were you at four o'clock, Mr Craig?'

Craig looked annoyed. 'Me? Why me?'

'It helps to know where everyone was at the time Maisie disappeared,' Millson said smoothly.

'Like I said, I was minding a stall in Station Yard.' His tone was surly.

'Thank you.' Millson heaved himself from the chair and stood up. Scobie closed his notebook. 'We'll get the search started right away, Mrs Brown.'

Carol jumped up from the sofa and seized his arm. 'What d'you think has happened to her?'

It wasn't the first time George Millson had looked into the red-rimmed eyes of a mother whose child was missing. And he didn't suppose it would be the last. He closed his mind against her torment. It was the only way he could work.

'That's what I have to find out. Try not to worry, Mrs Brown.'

The words were no help, but there was nothing he could say to ease Carol Brown's suffering. Only her doctor could do that, sedating her with drugs to blot out the agony.

Kathy Benson followed the two men out into the hall. 'Chief Inspector?'

'Yes?' Millson turned, his bulk filling the small entrance hall. He gazed into another pair of troubled eyes, though he had the feeling this girl was a stronger character than her sister.

'Last night, when I was out looking for Maisie, someone attacked me.' She told him about the incident at Alresford Creek.

'Apart from his arm round your neck and you fainting, did he do anything else?'

'No. But afterwards there was a boat on the river . . . I heard its outboard. I thought . . . well, I thought he might have Maisie and . . .'

'That's a mighty big assumption,' Millson said. 'D'you have any reason to think she was taken away by boat?'

'No, but it's a possibility, isn't it?'

'I'll keep it in mind.' His tone was kindly.

'And can you do anything about the press . . . and the television people? They're awful when something like this happens.'

She was right. In his experience a missing child brought the media out in force. They'd descend on family and neighbours like a pack of wolves, hounding them for information . . . photographs . . . interviews.

'I'll have a WPC stationed outside,' he promised. 'She'll look after things.'

He moved to the front door then paused with his hand on the latch. 'How did Maisie get on with Mr Craig?'

Startled by the unexpected question, Kathy hesitated between seeming disloyal to her sister and wanting to be helpful.

'Not all that well,' she said at last. 'Maisie still remembers her father, you see.' Dear, dead Alec with flowing golden hair like a Viking, who'd once promised to marry her.

Millson gave a grunt and lumbered out. Scobie followed him.

'Why did you lie to the police?' Carol Brown stared intently at Ronald Craig.

'What d'you mean?'

'You weren't at the stall when I went there to see if Maisie was with you.'

'I was taking a look round the fête.'

'Why didn't you tell the police that?'

'They didn't ask. Anyway, what's it matter? They're only interested in where I was at four o'clock. And I was at the stall then.'

'Were you?' Carol's voice was tense.

'Of course.'

Kathy said, 'They'll check, you know.'

'I don't need advice from you,' he said sourly. 'You keep your nose out of my affairs.'

'*Your* affairs?' She glared at him. 'Maisie is Carol's child, not yours. And she's *my* niece. This is *our* affair.'

'Oh yes, you're very good on affairs, aren't you?' he said nastily. 'Like your affair with Carol's husband.'

Kathy's face whitened with anger. 'There was no affair,' she said tautly.

'No?' He smiled unpleasantly. 'That's not the way I heard it.'

'Stop it, Ronnie!' Carol cried. 'Maisie's been taken. Can't you understand? Nothing else matters.'

At breakfast-time, Sidney Nunn received a phone call from Charles Cresswell.

'Everything go all right last night?'

'Yes, fine.'

'I hope you haven't kept any souvenirs. The place is crawling with police looking for this missing child. They'll be into everywhere, poking and prying.'

'My place is clean. What about your boatyard?'

'There's nothing there,' Cresswell said. 'But we'll have to suspend operations until this Maisie Brown business is over.'

Most of the houses in Tanniford were Victorian terrace houses, with a Tudor building here and there and a row of Georgian houses fronting the quay. PC Baxter's house opposite the post office—one of the handful of properties above the railway line—had been built as a police house and was modern.

In the office there, which served as the local police station, Millson briefed the sergeant leading the search. It began at ten o'clock with police from the county augmented by volunteers from the village.

At ten-thirty an articulated lorry backed into the concrete drive of the house and uncoupled a police trailer-van. Shortly after, a team of detectives, clerks and uniformed police arrived. By eleven o'clock an Incident Room had been set up complete with telephones, fax machine and a computer terminal. PC Baxter found himself relieved of his normal duties and attached to the Incident Room team.

'I want you to take the sergeant and me over the route this lass took yesterday afternoon,' Millson told him.

'Very good, sir.'

Baxter started at the entrance to the field where he'd set up the car park and led them across the bridge over the railway cutting and down the High Street. He stopped outside Nunn's newsagent's.

'This is where Maisie's friend, Vicki Calcot, says the two of them separated, sir. Vicki went inside the shop and Maisie walked on.' He moved on to the entrance to Blood Alley, a few yards further along. 'She'd have turned into this alleyway. It leads staight down to the back garden of her house.'

Millson peered into the gloom of Blood Alley. 'Anyone actually see her enter the alley?'

'Two or three people did, sir. She was very conspicuous in her majorettes's outfit.'

Millson stepped forward into the narrow alleyway, followed by the other two. 'All the world and his four wives have tramped along here since yesterday, I suppose,' he grumbled, scanning the ground.

'I'm afraid so, sir,' said Baxter.

'*Four* wives?' Scobie asked.

'Racist joke.' Millson didn't explain it to him.

At the rear of the shops they came to where Baker's Passage crossed the alley at right angles. Millson stopped and glanced up and down Baker's Passage in each direction before moving on.

Fifty yards further along Blood Alley they came to the back garden of Maisie Brown's home in Bath Street. From there, the alley continued between her house and the one next door to the street.

Millson turned about and walked back to the intersection of Blood Alley and Baker's Passage. He stood looking up and down Blood Alley.

'Let's assume she was snatched somewhere along this alleyway, between the High Street end and her house.' He scratched his face thoughtfully. 'Question is, was this man an opportunist who came upon her by chance? Or did he plan this, knowing she'd walk along here at that time?'

'I suppose it couldn't have been a woman?' Scobie ventured.

'Women snatch babies. They don't snatch eight-year-old girls,' Millson told him firmly. 'Except in custody cases—and this isn't one.' He turned to Baxter. 'Who uses these alleyways?'

'Mostly the High Street shopkeepers and the people who live in Bath Street.'

'Uh-huh. Now, you're the local lad . . . you know the

area. Where would he take her? Somewhere where he wouldn't be disturbed.'

'Perhaps the shipyard or the timber port, sir. They were closed and there'd be no one about on a Saturday afternoon. But he'd have to walk her through the crowds to get her to the shipyard and he'd be seen by lots of people. She'd be very conspicuous in that scarlet outfit.'

'And the timber port? Where's that?'

'You go down to the end of Baker's Passage here into West Street, sir,' Baxter told him. 'Opposite, there's a short street that leads to the timber yard and the river. He might take her across West Street to the yard without being seen, but the place would be locked. And there's a high wall round it.'

'He might have had keys.' Millson turned to Scobie. 'Didn't the stepfather say he works there?'

Scobie nodded.

'Get a frog team in to search the river,' Millson ordered. 'From above the timber port to below the shipyard.'

Baxter said quickly, 'The shipyard foreman syas she'd have been washed up on Osea Flats if she went in the river, sir.'

'Not if she was weighted with chain or stones, she wouldn't,' Millson said grimly. 'She'd be lying on the bottom here.'

Ted Baxter suddenly felt empty inside. Tanniford was a peaceful, law-abiding place, apart from some after-hours drinking and a few unlicensed cars. There was no real crime. Until this.

'What about empty houses . . . men living alone?' Millson asked.

'You'd best talk to Kathy Benson, sir,' said Baxter. 'She runs the estate agent's here . . . been in her family for years. She knows the ins and outs of every property in the village and who lives there. Better'n I do.'

'She's Carol Brown's sister . . . we met her this morning,'

Scobie reminded Millson. 'Attractive girl. Auburn hair, violet eyes . . .'

'Yes, I do know what she looks like,' Millson said heavily. 'When we've finished here you can go and see her. I want the addresses of empty properties, a note of who has the keys and a list of men in Tanniford living on their own.'

He looked around him. 'Now, let's suppose he attacks the girl here . . . maybe kills her, maybe not. Afterwards he drags or carries her away along one of these paths. Know what an eight-year-old girl weighs, Norris?'

'Afraid I don't,' Scobie said, not knowing any eight-year-old girls, let alone knowing one well enough to pick her up.

'My daughter weighed four and a half stone at that age—that's over sixty pounds.'

Scobie made no comment. Millson had mentioned his daughter only once before in the year they'd been working together and that was to choke Scobie off for asking about her. George Millson was divorced and his twelve-year-old daughter lived with his ex-wife. The wife had remarried and Millson bitterly resented having to arrange with her and the stepfather when he could see his daughter. Asking George about his wife or daughter was a bit like lighting a fuse, Scobie thought. An explosion was almost certain to follow.

'Which way would he take her?' Millson mused. 'Not back into the High Street among all the people. And probably not the other way, past her own house.' He pointed to the top end of Baker's Passage. 'What's up there?'

Baxter said, 'Station Road, sir. The High Street and the railway bridge are just to the right.'

'Let's take a look.' Millson strode up the passage and out into Station Road. He continued to the corner with the High Street and stood gazing across the bridge at the road out of Tanniford. He swung round.

'So, she could have been carried—or made to walk—to

the end of Baker's Passage . . . then put into a van or the boot of a car parked here in the street . . . and driven away out of the village.'

Baxter shook his head. 'No vehicle left Tanniford between the start of the fête and six o'clock when I lifted the barrier on the bridge.'

There was a sudden stillness in Millson. Scobie recognized the warning of a coming explosion.

'Say that again . . . slowly,' Millson said.

All at once Baxter felt guilty, as though he'd told a lie. Although the fact was, he reminded himself, the Chief Inspector hadn't asked him about vehicles before.

Nervously, he said, 'I put a barricade across the road at two p.m., sir. No vehicle entered or left Tanniford between then and six o'clock. And there's no other road out of the village.'

To Baxter's relief, Millson smiled. 'Good man. That's a great help. It means our man is almost certainly from the village. The girl's either still here or he hid her until the fête ended and took her out then.'

CHAPTER 3

They separated on the bridge, Millson and Baxter to return to the Incident Room, Scobie to see Kathy Benson. He'd assumed she'd still be at Carol Brown's house, but as he passed the window of the estate agent's on the corner of Station Road and the High Street, he saw her inside sitting at a desk. He pushed open the door and went in.

'Working on a Sunday, Miss Benson?'

Kathy looked up, attempting a smile. She'd taken the opportunity to escape from Ronald Craig's company and return to her office after Carol had been sedated by Doctor Osborne and ordered to rest.

'I have to do something to keep me occupied. I feel so useless,' Kathy said.

Scobie nodded understandingly. 'Well, here's a way you can help. The Chief Inspector would like the addresses of any empty properties in Tanniford.'

'Oh, that's easy enough. Take a seat.'

She reached for a pad of paper and began writing in neat, rounded characters. 'There are only three properties empty at the moment and I have the keys to them if you want to look inside,' she said.

She finished writing, tore off the sheet and handed it to him.

'Thank you,' Scobie said. 'There's some more information you may be able to give us. PC Baxter says you know the village pretty well.'

She nodded. 'I've lived here all my life. My father started the business forty years ago and I've worked in it for the last ten years. I've been into most of the houses here at one time or another and I think I know everyone.'

'So perhaps you could give me the names and addresses of any men living on their own.'

'Yes. No problem.' She ripped another sheet of paper from the pad. 'They're mostly elderly widowers and . . .' she smiled fleetingly, 'one or two deserted husbands.'

She began writing, pausing now and then to wrinkle her brows in concentration. Norris Scobie thought they were very nice eyebrows. She stopped writing and handed him the sheet of paper. He ran his eye down the list.

'You haven't put down Mr Turner,' he said.

She looked at him in astonishment. 'No, of course not.'

'Isn't his wife in hospital? That's what your sister said this morning.'

'Yes, but his son's there and . . .' She stopped. 'Well, if you're including men without a woman in the house, there are two more besides Ernie Turner and his son. There's a couple of gays living together in Ferry Street.' She took the list from him, wrote on it some more and handed it back.

'Were you working here yesterday while the fête was on?' Scobie asked.

'Yes, I'd given Gerald—Gerald Turner, my clerk . . . he's Mr Turner's son—the afternoon off to go and see his mother in hospital.'

'What was happening at the fête when Maisie was on her way home?'

'I have the programme here.' Kathy opened a drawer in her desk. 'Oh . . .' Her hand paused in the act of taking out the programme. 'I don't suppose you're interested in this.'

She picked up the thread of blue wool lying in the drawer and showed it to him. 'It caught in my nails while I was trying to stop that man choking me last night.'

'The Chief Inspector didn't think the incident was connected with Maisie's abduction,' Scobie said.

'No, I suppose not.' Kathy dropped the thread in the drawer and picked up the programme. She flicked through the pages. 'Here we are . . . the Tug of War. It started at three-thirty.'

'Where do they hold a tug of war in this small place?'

'On the river.' She smiled at his puzzled expression. 'It's quite narrow here. The teams are on opposite sides of the river and the winner is the one that pulls the other down into the mud. There were several teams taking part so it was probably still on at four o'clock.'

'D'you think I could have that programme?'

'Yes, of course.' She handed it to him.

He pocketed it. 'How long has Mr Craig been living with your sister?'

'About a year . . .' Kathy hesitated then went on, 'Carol went to pieces after she lost her husband. She desperately needed support . . . from anyone. Unfortunately, she chose Ronald Craig.'

'You don't like him?'

'No.'

Scobie waited for her to elaborate. When she didn't, he said, 'You told Mr Millson that Maisie didn't get along with her stepfather. Why was that?'

Kathy Benson hesitated again before answering. 'Maisie adored her father . . . wouldn't let Ronald take his place and . . . well, he's hardly the sort to win her over. Besides . . .' Kathy made a face, 'he's much too strict with her.'

'In what way?'

'When he smacks her . . . it's far too hard.'

She was silent for a moment, biting her lip and recalling past arguments with Ronald Craig over his treatment of Maisie. 'Look, I don't want to give the wrong impression, sergeant. I don't like Ronald Craig. I think he's a slob. But I don't believe he'd harm Maisie.'

Watching her expression, Scobie wondered how sure she was of that. 'Thank you, Miss Benson.' He stood up to go.

'Is there any news from the search?'

'I'm afraid not. We'd let you know immediately if there were.' Scobie looked into the violet eyes and wished he could allay the fear in them.

'I expect this sounds silly,' she said, 'but I make myself believe Maisie is alive and well. It's the only way I can keep going.'

It was a belief she'd tried to instil in Carol. 'You have to keep telling yourself Maisie is all right.'

'How *can* she be all right?' Carol had screamed at her hysterically.

'I don't know. But that's what we have to believe and hold onto. Otherwise we'll go mad.'

Kathy's voice was a whisper as she told Scobie, 'I really believe it.' Her eyes were moist.

'I believe it too,' he said recklessly, suddenly overcome by an urge to comfort her. He saw her eyes brighten.

'I'm glad you said that.' She smiled bravely.

After Scobie returned to the Incident Room with Kathy Benson's information, Millson called his team together and briefed them for the house-to-house inquiries.

On an enlarged street map of Tanniford pinned to the Incident Room wall, he traced Maisie Brown's route home with a pointer.

'She entered Blood Alley about four o'clock on the way to her house at the other end of the alley.' He ran the pointer round a circle he'd drawn on the map. 'This is an area within a fifty yards radius of the intersection of Blood Alley and Baker's Passage. Whoever snatched her didn't materialize out of thin air. He was *here*—' he thumped the map with his hand, 'inside this circle, at four o'clock. My guess is there were about a hundred people in that area yesterday, including the shops and houses. Only forty or so would have been men . . . the rest women and children.'

He paused to light a cigarette from the stub of the one he was smoking, then went on to tell them Tanniford had been sealed off to traffic yesterday afternoon and everyone was on foot. For this reason he believed Maisie Brown had been taken by someone in the village. Tanniford was a small place where people knew each other. Most of them had been out on the streets while the fête was on and so, in spite of the influx of visitors, he expected to be able to establish where everyone was at the time the girl disappeared.

'That's the immediate task,' Millson told the assembled officers. 'To ascertain where everyone was at four o'clock yesterday. All those in the vicinity of Blood Alley . . . I want to know their exact location. Who they were with. Who they saw. Our objective is to identify every person inside that circle on the map—particularly the men. We'll be using the electors' lists as a guide, but make sure you account for everyone in the house who was here yesterday.'

He drew heavily on his cigarette and blew out smoke through his nostrils. 'That's about it. Sergeant Scobie will give you your assignments. The keys of empty properties can be borrowed from the estate agent's on the corner of Station Road and the High Street. Scobie and I will be interviewing the men living alone. Any questions?' He looked around. 'No? Good. When you report back here, pass your information to the collator.'

While Scobie was handing out the assignments, Millson spoke to the uniformed sergeant in charge of the Operations Room.

'I want a large scale diagram made of that area around Blood Alley and put up on the wall,' he told him. 'And as the information comes in, I want it marked to show where everyone was when this kiddie was snatched.'

The sergeant nodded. 'Right, sir. We'll use red pins for men, yellow for women, green for children.'

'Fine.' Millson glanced across the room. 'Is the computer terminal working?'

'Yes, sir.'

'Tell the operator to open a file, "fête-day population" and a sub-file, "Blood Alley area". I want every entry linked to a coloured pin on the map showing that person's location at four o'clock yesterday.'

After the briefing, Millson issued a statement to the media. He gave the bare details of Maisie Brown's disappearance and handed out facsimile copies of her picture. The police feared for her safety, he said. They were making house-to-house inquiries and a search was in progress. He appealed for anyone with information, or who was in Tanniford on Saturday afternoon, to come forward or to phone the Incident Room.

When Millson finished with the reporters Scobie told him what Kathy Benson had said about Ronald Craig. 'She doesn't think he would actually harm the child, though.'

Millson's face darkened. 'He already has, hasn't he? He's hit her hard enough for Miss Benson to worry about.' He sucked in his cheeks. 'Have a DC check Craig's story. See if he was at that stall in Station Yard all afternoon as he says he was.'

Millson and Scobie started on Kathy Benson's list with the two men living closest to Blood Alley, one in Station Road, the other in West Street. The first man was crippled with arthritis and could scarcely walk. The second was eighty-four.

'Neither of 'em would have the inclination, let alone the strength,' said Millson, crossing off their names.

The next name was Ernie Turner's. His son, Gerald, answered the door at the address in Spring Street. Gerald Turner was seventeen. He had dark wavy hair and large brown eyes with the longest eyelashes Scobie had ever seen on a boy. He had a soft, rounded face and his complexion was flawless. 'Pretty', was the word Scobie later wrote in his notebook.

In a low voice, Gerald told them his father was at the hospital. 'My mother's dying of cancer. She's not expected to live much longer.'

Millson made rumbling noises in his throat meant to convey sympathy. 'I understand your father knew Maisie Brown quite well,' he said.

'I wouldn't know. You'd best ask him.' Gerald Turner's tone was suddenly sharp.

'Oh I will.' Millson's tone was equally sharp. 'Meantime, d'you mind telling us where *you* were yesterday afternoon?'

The brown eyes widened slightly. 'Miss Benson gave me the afternoon off to visit my mother. I was at the Essex county hospital in Colchester.'

'Uh-huh. Did you know Maisie yourself?'

'Only to say "hallo" to.'

'What about when she came to the house?'

'She came to see my father, not me. I don't play with little girls.'

Millson raised his eyebrows. 'No, I don't suppose you do,' he said. 'Well, thank you for your time, Gerald, and when your father gets back, ask him to call in at the Incident Room right away.' He turned to leave, then turned back again. 'Sorry about your mum,' he said awkwardly.

'Thank you.' Gerald Turner's eyes glistened with tears as he closed the door.

The next two men Millson and Scobie called on gave satisfactory explanations of their whereabouts on Saturday afternoon, supported by details of who they'd been with and who they'd been seen by.

The last three addresses on Kathy Benson's list were in Ferry Street. There was no reply from the first.

'They're away,' a neighbour told them. 'Richard and Bernard always spend the summer in San Francisco.'

The next address was opposite. The occupant, Frank Belmer, worked at Cresswell Marine managing Cresswell's fleet of hire cruisers. He told them he wasn't in Tanniford on Saturday. In fact, he hadn't been in Tanniford from Friday evening to Sunday morning. He'd been in Brightlingsea. He supplied names of people who would verify that.

The last man, Holy Joe, lived in what had once been a grocer's shop on the corner of Ferry Road and East Street. Baxter had warned them he was an odd character.

'Well-educated . . . comes from a good family . . . but he's got religion in a big way. Reckons his mission in life is to save the world.'

Holy Joe opened the door to them wearing a Russian sailor's hat. Around the hatband, instead of a ship's name, were the words GOD IS LOVE in gold letters. His face was chubby and smiling and he wore round, steel-framed spectacles.

He showed them into a front room which had been the original shop. It was bare except for an old organ against the wall and a row of wooden chairs. Scobie and Millson sat on two of the chairs and Holy Joe sat with his back to the organ on the bench seat. The entire population of the fête were witness to his movements, he told them.

'I saw everyone and everyone saw me,' he said proudly.

'How was that, Mr-er . . . Joe?' Millson asked.

'Because, Mr Policeman, I blessed some three hundred souls with the Lord's Word.'

'Really? How did you do that?'

Holy Joe gave Millson a hurt look as though he'd expected him to know. 'Why, as I always do . . . by handing out my texts and putting them on cars.'

'Cars?' Millson's eyes flickered with sudden interest.

'Yes, I put a leaflet on every car and van . . . under the windscreen wiper. It doesn't blow away then.'

Millson exchanged glances with Scobie. 'That's very interesting, Mr-er . . . look, what *is* your name?' Kathy Benson had simply written 'Holy Joe' against his address.

'Everyone calls me Holy Joe. I'm happy with that.'

'Just for the record, though?' Scobie asked.

Holy Joe said in a lofty tone, 'Montague Pratt.'

'Thank you, Mr Pratt,' said Millson. 'D'you think you'd remember where these vehicles were parked?'

'Of course. They belong to people in the village.'

'In that case it would be a help—a great help—if you'd come up to the Incident Room and show us on our street map exactly where they were parked yesterday afternoon.'

Holy Joe frowned. 'Plenty of other people saw them.'

'Yes, but you're the only person who saw them *all*,' Millson insisted. He saw Holy Joe hesitating. 'Your information is vital to our inquiries,' he said.

Holy Joe looked up at the ceiling. 'Then I think God would want me to help.'

'I'm sure he would,' Millson said solemnly. 'And while we're here, d'you think God would mind if we took a look around . . . just to make sure this little girl hasn't hidden herself somewhere in your house?'

'My house is your house,' Holy Joe said gravely. 'Please look wherever you wish.'

On the map in the Incident Room, Holy Joe pointed out where vehicles had been parked the previous afternoon. The clerk who was map plotting marked their positions and another clerk logged the owners as Holy Joe named them. Only one vehicle was near the exit from Baker's Passage into Station Road and that was the van belonging to Nunn's the newsagent's. 'He usually parks it outside his shop in the High Street,' Holy Joe said.

The search for Maisie Brown was called off at nightfall. The village, the shipyard and the timber port had been searched again and then Tanniford woods above the village and the countryside beyond. Several items of clothing had been found. None of them belonged to Maisie. And the police frogmen had found nothing in the river.

*

That night Millson and Scobie snatched a few hours' sleep in Ted Baxter's spare room. During the day his wife, Barbara, had kept them supplied with food and drink. The rest of the staff were catered for by a mobile police canteen that appeared next to the Incident Room at midday and then drove off to supply the search parties.

As he drifted off to sleep, Millson remembered Ernie Turner hadn't turned up at the Incident Room to see him. Perhaps he was still at the hospital with Mrs Turner. Millson decided to call at the house again in the morning.

But on Monday morning Ernie Turner killed himself.

MONDAY

CHAPTER 4

When sixty-six-year-old Ernie Turner jumped out of the top window of his three storey house in Spring Street, a few hours after his wife died, everyone thought it was because he couldn't bear to live without her. He'd often said as much to people.

Ernie had returned from hospital while his son was at work. Soon after, he mounted the stairs to the top of the house. He opened a window and looked up and down the street to make sure no one was about. Then he climbed out onto the sill.

Ernie had intended to go to his death quietly. As he launched himself into space, however, the reality of the hard stone pavement below flashed into his mind and he screamed in terror. His scream brought out old Alice, who'd been sitting in the porch of her cottage a few doors away. She was just in time to see Ernie land, his head hitting the pavement with the sound of a loud smack.

Unhurriedly, she ambled out of her gate and along the street to where he lay. Alice was ninety-two. She'd outlived three husbands and two of her five children. She'd been a nurse in the Second World War and she had no fear of death. Stooping down, she pressed a finger to the side of Ernie's neck. There was no pulse. She straightened and shuffled along the street to the Black Dog.

The barman looked up in surprise as she entered. Although the Black Dog opened early in the morning for the first shift at the shipyard, Alice never came in for her tot of brandy before midday. She would sit in a corner making it last until the shipyard workers came in at lunchtime and bought her another for old times' sake. Alice's last husband had worked in the yard and was still remembered there by some of the workers

'You're early, Alice. The usual?' the barman asked.

'Make it a double,' she said. 'An' get someone to run up the road to Benson's an' tell young Gerry his da's just jumped out the window an' he's dead. Better tell Ted Baxter an' all.'

Gerald Turner reached the house a few minutes before PC Baxter. It was long enough for him to find and read the letter his father had left on the kitchen table and pocket it.

Baxter inspected the body and satisfied himself Ernie Turner was dead. He turned to Alice who'd downed her brandy and returned to the scene. 'You saw him jump?'

'No, I heard him yell. Time I got out he'd hit the street.'

Baxter nodded and wrote in his notebook. 'I wonder why he yelled.'

'Changed his mind, I 'spect. They do sometimes,' Alice said knowingly.

An ambulance arrived. Watched by his son and a handful of villagers, Ernie Turner's body was loaded into the ambulance and driven away.

Gerald Turner went into the house. Baxter followed him. 'Sorry about this, lad. And about your mum too. I gather she died this morning.'

'Yes. Dad was with her at the end.'

'Came straight home and did this?'

'Yes.'

'Did he leave a note?'

'No.'

'You've looked?'

'Yes.'

Baxter tapped his teeth with the end of his pencil. 'Odd that. They usually do.'

'Dad wasn't much of a one for writing things.'

'No, you're right there. Was there any other reason he might have done it? Anything on his mind?'

'No.' Gerald Turner spoke with sudden emphasis.

Baxter looked at him. The boy was white-faced. Shock, he assumed. He closed his notebook and replaced it in his breast pocket. 'Right, that seems clear enough then. I'll make my report. There'll have to be an inquest.'

'Inquest?' Gerald Turner looked startled.

'Oh yes, there has to be. Not natural causes, see? Don't worry about it. The coroner won't talk about his balance of mind being disturbed. Not these days. He'll most likely say he was terribly upset over your mother's death and took his own life.'

Old Ernie might have considered what this would do to his son, though, what with his mother's death as well, Baxter thought, observing the haunted expression in Gerald Turner's eyes.

The Incident Room was at full stretch when PC Baxter returned. Maisie Brown's abduction had been reported in Monday morning's papers and on Sunday evening's television news. It brought a flood of phone calls to the Incident Room from people who had been at the fête on Saturday. There were personal callers as well, villagers anxious to give information. Two collators and a map plotter worked flat out to keep abreast of the information pouring in. Another collator processed the reports of Sunday afternoon's house-to-house inquiries by Millson's team of detectives.

'No suicide note?'

Millson frowned when Baxter reported Ernie Turner's leap to his death. In his experience, most people didn't depart for the next world without saying why. Ernie Turner had been very friendly with Maisie Brown. He might have had another reason, apart from the death of his wife, for ending his life. Millson decided to question Gerald Turner again about Maisie's visits to his father.

Before then, the detective-constable assigned to check Ronald Craig's movements on Saturday reported in.

'Craig wasn't at the stall all the time, sir,' the DC told him. 'Two of the stallholders say he was absent for about an hour between three-thirty and five.'

'Was he now?' Millson's nostrils flared. 'In that case I want to talk to Mr Craig!'

George Millson's office was a tiny room at one end of the police trailer. Craig looked nervous as he sat down at the small table almost nose-to-nose with Millson. Scobie, cramped between the side of the table and the wall, opened his notebook.

Millson hunched forward, his bulk dwarfing Craig. 'Yesterday you told me you were minding a stall in Station Yard on Saturday afternoon.'

'That's right.'

Millson watched people's eyes when he was questioning them. Craig's eyes were darting this way and that, trying to avoid him.

'Weren't there all the time though, were you?'

'No.' Craig looked uncomfortable. 'I went for a look round the fête for a while.'

'When was that?'

'I didn't notice the exact time.'

'Roughly, then.'

'About four o'clock.'

Millson leaned back in his chair. 'I'm puzzled, you see, Mr Craig. Out there on the wall we have a map. It has a lot of pins stuck in it. Every pin is a person. Lots of people seeing lots of other people . . . telling us who they were, who they saw, who they were with.' He leaned forward again. 'No one has reported seeing you.'

'I wasn't around very long,' Craig muttered. 'Just stretching me legs.'

Millson eased his bulk away from the table and managed

to open a drawer. He took out a photocopied diagram and slapped it on the table in front of Craig.

'That's a street map of Tanniford, Mr Craig. I'd like you to show us just exactly where you went on this walkabout of yours.'

Craig stared at the map. Slowly his finger traced a route out of Station Yard, along West Street into Chapel Street and back again. He looked up and braved Millson's eyes for an instant.

'That's where I walked,' he said defiantly.

'That's nowhere near the fête itself.'

'That's why no one saw me.'

Millson said nothing, hunching his shoulders higher until his head seemed enclosed between them. Craig looked down at the table. Scobie studied his notes. The silence dragged on.

Millson's shoulders dropped back into place. 'I'm not satisfied with that explanation,' he said bluntly. 'I suggest you reconsider it.'

Craig raised his head. His face was blank. He pulled a packet of cigarettes from his pocket. 'Mind if I smoke?' He started to extract one from the packet.

'Yes, I do,' Millson said curtly. 'This is a very small room and my sergeant here suffers with asthma.'

Scobie controlled his face. He didn't have asthma and George Millson was a twenty a day man who didn't give a damn about the room being filled with smoke.

'Oh . . . sorry,' Craig mumbled. He lowered his head again, eyes downcast. Millson sat motionless. After a while Craig said, 'All right, I'll tell you where I was. I was with someone.'

'Who?'

'A woman.'

Millson arched his eyebrows at Scobie. Not that old standby, his expression said.

Craig lifted his eyes and caught Millson's reaction. He

went on quickly, 'I realize you'll have to check. I hope you'll be discreet 'cos she's married. Her husband owns the fish and chip shop in East Street.'

'Her name and address?' Millson asked coldly.

'Betsy Sparrow. She lives in Chapel Street—where I showed you on the map. I was with her from about four o'clock until five. She'll confirm.'

'Where was her husband?'

'Down on the quay. He had a stall there selling seafood.'

'And where will we find Mrs Sparrow at the moment?'

'She'll be at the shop.' Craig's face showed alarm. 'Look, I don't want you going to the shop. Can't she come here?'

'No,' Millson said brusquely. 'We won't interview her in front of her husband, though. For her sake, not yours,' he added sourly.

Craig nodded and rose from the chair. 'I haven't finished!' Millson snapped. Craig sank into the chair again like a balloon deflating.

'Do you like little Maisie?' Millson asked.

Craig was thrown by the question. 'Yes . . . of course . . . what d'you mean?'

'Do you *love* her?'

He looked uncomfortable. 'Yes, I suppose so.'

Millson said softly, 'And yet you beat her.'

Craig's eyes flashed with alarm. 'I give her a good smacking when she's cheeky. That's all. I don't beat her . . . don't use a stick.'

'Oh, I'm glad to hear that.' Millson's voice dripped sarcasm.

'I suppose Carol's sister's been yacking to you.' Craig's tone was surly. 'You don't want to take notice of her. She hates me.'

'Why's that?'

Craig shrugged. 'Doesn't think I'm good enough for Carol, I expect.' He smirked nastily. 'Or could be she's jealous . . . maybe like to be in her place. She tried to make it with Carol's husband, you know.'

Scobie stopped writing notes, hot with anger. He didn't believe Kathy Benson was the kind of girl to have an affair with her sister's husband.

'When was this?' he jerked out and saw Millson glance at him in surprise, wondering at the relevance of the question.

'Just before he drowned hisself.'

'You mean he committed suicide?'

Craig smiled unpleasantly. 'Well, they said it was an accident . . . but Carol thinks he did. Broke her up, you know.'

Scobie clamped his teeth together, fighting the temptation to hit Craig and knock the sneering smile from his face.

'That's all for the moment, Mr Craig,' said Millson.

CHAPTER 5

It was lunch-time and Fred Sparrow and his wife were busy serving shipyard workers. Millson and Scobie stood out among them like nuns at a football match as they pushed their way through the crush to the counter.

The heat in the shop—with a warm July day outside, the fish fryers and the throng of customers inside—was overbearing. Behind the counter, Betsy Sparrow's white linen overall was unfastened top and bottom, barely held together by two buttons in the middle. As she bent forward wrapping orders, it gaped open to expose the top of her breasts. And when she turned round to shovel a trowel of chips into a bag for the next customer, the overall parted high on a bare thigh. Betsy Sparrow was naked beneath her overall.

She was mid-thirties, a vivacious woman, with shoulder-length dark hair. She greeted every male customer with a wide smile and when she'd served him she sent him on his way with an even wider one.

'No wonder business is good,' Millson murmured as they stood watching her.

Betsy looked up and saw them. Her eyes flicked up and down their suits. She gave them the same warm smile as she gave the customers and wiped her hands on a cloth.

'I'll deal with these gentlemen, Fred,' she told her husband. She lifted a flap at the end of the counter and motioned the two police officers to a door at the rear of the shop.

It led to a storeroom. There was nowhere to sit. Betsy closed the door and leaned back against it.

'How can I help you gentlemen?' Her voice was deep and husky.

'I'm Chief Inspector Millson and this is Sergeant Scobie,' Millson said.

'Yes, I know . . . everyone in the village knows.' She treated them to another dazzling smile. Betsy Sparrow exuded friendliness and warmth. When she smiled at you, you automatically smiled back, Scobie discovered.

'I understand Mr Craig spent some time with you on Saturday afternoon,' Millson said.

'That's right.' Her eyes met his boldly.

'What time was this?'

'Oh . . . between four and five.'

'Can you be more precise?'

Her dark eyebrows came together in concentration. 'He left about ten to five—'cos I went down the quay at five. Saturday afternoon's me afternoon off and I told Fred straight, fête or no fête, I wasn't working on me afternoon off, but I'd help him clear up. Now . . .' She placed a forefinger on her lower lip and concentrated harder. 'When did Ronnie *come*?' She giggled. 'To the house, I mean.' She shook her head. 'Can't be exact. I reckon about half an hour or so before.'

'You can't say for certain he was with you at four o'clock, then?' Millson said.

Scobie watched her grasp the significance of the time. The smile went from her face as suddenly as a light being turned off. She let out a little gasp. 'You can't think Ronnie had anything to do with—' She broke off. 'No . . . that's too terrible . . .'

'Yes or no please, Mrs Sparrow,' said Millson.

'No,' she whispered.

'Have you known Mr Craig long?'

'Six months.'

'And you meet frequently?'

'About twice a week.'

'Does Mrs Brown know of your association?'

'No! Of course not.' Betsy sounded horrified. 'She'd be

devastated. Look . . .' She bit her lower lip. 'I wouldn't hurt Carol. She's a nice girl—too good for Ronnie. I haven't broken up a happy relationship or anything like that, you know. He's using her as a convenience . . . somewhere to live when his wife chucked him out. Carol knows that.'

'D'you think he was fond of Maisie?'

She considered the question. 'I honestly don't know,' she said. 'He never mentioned her.'

'What does a woman like Betsy Sparrow see in a creep like Craig?' Scobie asked as they walked up the High Street.

'Don't be naïve, Norris,' Millson said. 'It's not what a man looks like to a woman, it's what he does in bed that matters.'

He paused at the entrance to Blood Alley and gazed down it. 'It's only a short step from Maisie's house to Chapel Street,' he said. 'Craig had time to attack her at home before he went to Betsy's.'

'Yes, but why would he?' Scobie asked.

'Perhaps she knew about his visits to Betsy Sparrow and threatened to tell her mum. He didn't like the child and she certainly didn't like him. If he didn't want to lose his comfortable berth with Carol he'd have to silence her.'

'Murder her to keep a roof over his head? Stretching things a bit, isn't it?'

'He might not have meant to kill her—only to frighten her—and lost his temper. He's a nasty piece of work.'

Scobie shook his head doubtfully. 'You just don't like stepfathers, George.'

It slipped out accidentally and he could have bitten his tongue off. Stepfathers were a taboo subject because of Millson's difficulties with his daughter's stepfather.

But Millson merely growled, 'I don't like stepfathers who beat their stepdaughters.'

They walked on and after a few steps he added, 'Anyway, you don't like him either.'

'*Touché*.' Scobie grinned.

'*Touché?* I suppose that's your French ancestry coming out,' Millson said waspishly.

Nearing the estate agent's he said, 'Let's have a word with Gerald Turner. I want to ask him about Maisie and his father.'

'It's not a very good time, is it? His dad's just committed suicide.'

'That's what bothers me. He knew we wanted to interview him and he goes and jumps out the window. And doesn't leave a note.'

'But the man's dead!'

'Norris, I had them check CRO this morning. Turner was a flasher. He had a conviction for indecent exposure.'

Millson tried the door of Benson's Estate Agency. It was locked and a sign on the door said CLOSED.

'Round her sister's, I expect,' he said, turning to walk down the High Street.

'I don't think so.' Across in the churchyard Scobie saw a figure standing by a gravestone. 'She's over there.'

Millson squinted in the direction of Scobie's finger. 'Well, go and ask her where young Turner is.'

Scobie crossed the road and entered the churchyard gates. Threading his way between the gravestones, he made for the solitary figure of Kathy Benson.

Kathy gazed at the headstone with misty eyes. She usually visited Alec's grave on the anniversary of his death and at Christmas. Today was a special visit.

Look after Maisie for me. Those had been his last words to her before that fatal trip. She'd felt a guilty pleasure in his trust. It wasn't that Carol was a bad mother—she loved Maisie dearly—but she was impetuous and Alec liked Kathy to watch over her when he was away at sea.

Kathy hadn't known about the dreadful quarrel till afterwards. The morning he left Alec had told Carol he was in love with Kathy and wanted a divorce.

It had been a story of two sisters wanting the same man and the younger one trapping him. One night after a village dance, the eager, predatory Carol enticed Alec into a situation beyond his control. A month later she told him, triumphantly, she was pregnant.

Alec married her and a desolated Kathy buried her love and sought distraction in her father's estate agency business.

Two years ago, Alec told Kathy he'd tried to make the marriage work for Maisie's sake, but it was a failure. He asked Kathy whether she would marry him if her were free. She had said yes, but she didn't want Carol hurt more than necessary.

The weather in the North Sea was bad on that last voyage. As the men hauled in the nets, Alec, manning the trawler's stern winch, was swept overboard by a rogue wave and drowned.

'It was your fault!' Carol screamed at Kathy. 'His mind wasn't on what he was doing. We'd quarrelled all night . . . over *you*! I never want to speak to you again!'

The rift might have healed if Carol hadn't taken Ronald Craig into her home a year later. Kathy was appalled her sister could turn to another man so soon after Alec's death and the alienation between them deepened. It had taken the shock of Maisie's abduction to bring them together.

Kathy had a special feeling for Maisie. Maisie was the child she and Alec might have had if things had been different. Maisie had walked right past her door that afternoon with her friend Vicki. If Kathy hadn't been so busy . . . had looked out and seen her . . . called her in . . .

Kathy laid a hand on the headstone. 'I'm so sorry, Alec,' she whispered. 'I'll find her. I'll get her back.'

She heard a sound behind her. Startled, she whirled round. Scobie had coughed to attract her attention.

'I'm sorry to disturb you.' He stepped up beside her and read the inscription on the headstone. *Alec, beloved husband of Carol . . .*

'Someone you were fond of?' he asked casually.

'Yes . . . once . . . Maisie's father.'

Scobie lowered his eyes. What Craig had said was true. The tragic expression on Kathy Benson's face confirmed it.

'We'd like to speak to Gerald Turner,' he said in a formal voice. 'Can you tell us where he is?'

'Yes, he's at home. I told him to take as much time off as he liked. It's been a terrible shock for him . . . losing both parents at once like that.'

Gerald Turner's boyish face was creased with misery when he opened the door. Even George Millson was moved.

'Sorry to hear about your father's death,' he rumbled. 'Mind if I ask you some questions about it?'

'No. Come in.' Gerald showed them into a bright, modern-looking sitting-room.

As they sank into armchairs of soft black leather Millson looked around appraisingly. 'Nice room.'

'My mother designed it. She liked nice things.' Scobie heard the catch in his voice.

'Uh-huh. Your father was pretty upset by her death, was he?'

'Yes. That's why he killed himself.' Gerald Turner sat down on the sofa, sitting forward on the edge.

'Sure of that, are you?'

'How d'you mean?'

'Well, if he didn't leave a note, how can you be sure why he did it?'

'Well, it's obvious that was the reason.'

'Nothing's obvious to me, son,' Millson growled. 'Tell me about your dad and little Maisie Brown.'

Gerald Turner looked startled by the question. 'There's

nothing to tell. She came here sometimes . . . he played games with her and—'

'What sort of games?'

'Kid's games. Happy Families . . . Snap . . . that sort of thing. And sometimes he read to her. She loved him to read stories to her.'

Millson glanced at Scobie. 'Alone together a lot, were they?'

Gerald Turner said sharply, 'Yes, I suppose so. What are you getting at?'

Brutally, Millson said, 'Your father had a conviction for indecency with a young girl.'

You're a real sod, George, Scobie thought. It had been eight years ago, the girl was nineteen and Turner had been put on probation.

Millson watched unmoved as the youth's face crumpled. 'Why bring that up? It was years ago . . . before we moved here. He never did it again.'

'So far as you know.'

Scobie looked up from his notebook. The boy was on the verge of tears. Scobie wondered whether Millson's hardness came from years of dealing with crime or from bitterness over his wife leaving him. Probably the latter. Scobie believed, deep down, George Millson was a scarred man.

Gerald Turner said in a low voice, 'You have no right to say that.'

Millson ignored the protest. 'Are you absolutely certain your father didn't leave a note? A letter perhaps?'

'I've looked everywhere and I'm positive.' The soft brown eyes met Millson's hard blue ones without wavering.

'Any idea where he was at four o'clock on Saturday?'

Gerald Turner's eyes widened. Everyone in the village knew that was when Maisie Brown vanished. 'You suspect my father!'

'It's a routine question we ask about everyone,' Millson said.

'Oh . . . well, I expect he would have been on his way to the hospital to visit my mother. We took it in turns to be with her—we knew she was dying, you see.' Suddenly his eyes filled with tears and he turned away.

Stolidly, Millson said, 'According to witnesses he was still watching the majorettes' parade at half past three. What time did he relieve you at the hospital?'

Gerald Turner hesitated. 'About seven o'clock, I think.'

'Uh-huh.' Millson was silent for a while. Then with a grunt he heaved himself to his feet. 'I'd like to take a look around while we're here.'

Scobie closed his notebook and stood up too. They had no right to search, but Millson had made his request sound like an order and Turner was too young and vulnerable to challenge it.

Gerald did seem about to object, however. 'No, I . . .' He wavered. 'Yes, OK. Go ahead.'

He followed them from room to room. Upstairs, when they crossed the landing to a rear bedroom, he moved ahead and stood in the doorway.

'This is my room,' he said, as though not expecting them to enter.

Millson pushed past him. Scobie following, took in the dressing-table, the delicate colours and furnishings. He opened a cupboard. It was filled with men's clothes. Millson opened the wardrobe next to it. Dresses and skirts hung on the rails.

'My mother kept some of her things in here,' Gerald Turner said quickly.

'That your mother?' Millson pointed to a framed black and white photograph on the dressing-table.

'Yes.'

Millson picked it up. *All my love darling, Rachel* was scrawled in the corner. Millson was an ardent watcher of silent films. The young woman with dark, Cleopatra-style hair, was the image of his idol, Louise Brooks. He replaced the photograph.

'Your mother was very attractive.'

'She was beautiful.' Gerald Turner spoke proudly.

'Younger than your father, I imagine.'

'Much younger.'

Scobie heard the emphasis in his tone and wondered about Gerald Turner's relationship with his mother.

On their way out of the room he noticed the broken door catch and the handle hanging loose.

'Has someone forced the door?'

'It jammed,' Turner said. 'I broke the lock getting it open.'

'He was lying,' Millson said as they walked away from the house. 'He lied about the door and he lied about there being no note. I saw it in his eyes.'

'A bit hard on him about his father though, weren't you?'

'I don't have time for sentiment, Norris. I was trying to find out if the old man jumped out of remorse or guilt for something he'd done to Maisie. His son's hiding something and I'd like to know what it is.'

Sitting in his bedroom, Gerald Turner worried over what he'd said about the damaged door. Any explanation had been better than the truth. He always kept the door locked. That morning, after returning from hospital, his father had broken into the room and searched the drawers and cupboards.

Then he'd written that terrible letter and killed himself.

CHAPTER 6

On their way back from Gerald Turner's, Millson called on Carol Brown in Bath Street. He felt it important to maintain her confidence and he had a couple of questions to ask her.

Carol was lying on the sofa in the front room, propped up with cushions. Kathy Benson was squatting on the floor beside the sofa holding her sister's hand. She'd closed the business for the day when she sent Gerald Turner home, and after visiting the churchyard she'd come on to Carol's house.

She gave Scobie a quick smile of acknowledgement. There was no sign of Ronald Craig. Scobie presumed he'd returned to work after his interview with Millson.

Millson drew up a chair and sat down beside the sofa. Carol's face was pasty and she'd aged years since he spoke to her yesterday. She turned glazed eyes upon him. That would be the sedatives the doctor had given her, he reckoned.

'Is there any news?' Her voice was listless.

He shook his head. 'Not yet. I wanted to ask you about Mr Turner.'

'Yes, Kathy told me about it . . . poor Gerald.'

'Strange he didn't leave a note.' Millson's eyes encompassed both sisters.

'Not really,' Kathy said. 'He worshipped Rachel. If you lose someone you love very much . . . beside yourself with grief and can't go on . . . I don't think you stop to write notes about it.'

'Maybe not.' Millson sounded unconvinced. 'What was Mr Turner like?' he asked Carol.

'A dear old man. He was very kind to Maisie.'

'She never expressed any worries about him?'

'Worries?' Carol looked puzzled. 'No. She loved going to see him.'

Scobie saw Kathy frown and prayed Millson wouldn't mention Turner's conviction. These two had enough to worry about without adding that. With relief he heard Millson say, 'Yes, that's what his son told us.' He went on, 'Was there any other man Maisie was particularly friendly with?'

She sighed wearily. 'Not that I know of.'

'H'm.' Millson was thoughtful for a moment. Then he asked, 'Is there anyone who might have a grudge against you?'

'You think Maisie was taken as some kind of revenge against Carol?' Kathy asked incredulously.

'I have to consider every possibility,' Millson said.

Carol shook her head. 'I can't think of anyone.'

'There's just one more question,' he said. 'Can you be sure Maisie didn't come into the house on Saturday?'

She frowned. 'Yes, I think so. Because the back door key was still in its hiding place and her majorette's outfit wasn't here.'

'Thank you.' Millson stood up to leave.

Carol Brown's face folded. 'You think Maisie's dead, don't you,' she said dully.

He bent down and to Scobie's astonishment took her hands in his. 'No, Carol, I don't,' he said firmly. 'I don't have a single fact to make me think she's dead. Nothing. You understand?'

She stared up at him with haunted eyes and nodded dumbly.

Some time after they left, Kathy's memory was jogged by one of the Chief Inspector's questions.

'What about Bobby North, Carol? He has good reason to hate you, doesn't he?'

'Oh, Kathy . . . don't be silly.' Carol's tone was listless. 'Besides, he's in prison.'

On their return to the Incident Room, Millson perused the latest reports. At three o'clock he issued a second statement to waiting reporters.

He told them Maisie Brown had been missing for forty-eight hours now and he was increasingly worried for her safety. An extensive police search had found no trace of her and inquiries were continuing. Anyone who was in Tanniford on Saturday afternoon should come forward, or ring the Incident Room, if they had not already done so.

Shortly after, Scobie put his head round the door of Millson's office and said he had a visitor. 'She's the choir-mistress from the church.'

'What's her name?'

'Humm.'

Millson arched his eyebrows. 'Is that a joke, Norris?'

'No. It's her name . . . Gladys Humm.'

'Bring her in.'

Gladys Humm was a middle-aged spinster. She wore a grey cardigan over a grey skirt and her brown hair was done in a bun. The rimless spectacles sat on her nose at an angle, giving her a drunken appearance.

Cramped into the tiny room with the two police officers, Miss Humm found herself—like Ronald Craig before her—nose-to-nose with George Millson when she sat down at the table. She dropped her eyes in embarrassment and they fell upon the thick black hairs on the backs of his hands. Embarrassed still further, she quickly raised her eyes again to the level of his chin.

'You have something to tell us, Miss Humm?'

Gladys Humm's Adam's apple bobbed as she swallowed and said yes, she had. She'd been standing by the gates to the churchyard a minute or so before four o'clock yesterday. She was sure of the time because she was meeting two of the choirboys at four o'clock and she'd looked at her watch.

She'd seen Maisie Brown and her friend Vicki Calcot on the opposite side of the High Street, outside Sidney Nunn's sweetshop.

'They were arguing about something,' she said. 'Then

Vicki went into the shop and Maisie walked on and turned into Blood Alley.'

'You actually saw her go into the alley?'

'Oh, yes.'

'Was she alone?'

'Yes.'

'Did you notice anyone follow her?'

'No, but the choirboys arrived just then so I wasn't watching. Someone could have done.'

Millson nodded. 'Miss Humm, I'd like you to try and remember every person you saw in the High Street at that time.'

'Oh dear.' Her eyes lifted and met his in alarm. 'There were so many. The street was full of people.'

'Just take your time.'

Despite her doubts, Gladys Humm had total recall and a near-photographic memory. As she began to describe the people around her, Scobie quickly made a sketch map of the High Street and marked their positions.

She finished and said, 'I must be the last person to see her alive, mustn't I, Chief Inspector?' She dipped her head to look at him through the top half of her bi-focals.

'Miss Humm, we have no evidence that Maisie is dead,' he said severely.

'Oh, no . . . no, of course not. But—'

'Is there anything else you can tell us?'

She hesitated. There was the matter of some items stolen from the costume wardrobe of the Tanniford Players in the village hall. However, the police were too busy with this poor child's disappearance to be bothered with thefts from the local amateur dramatic society, she told herself. She shook her head. 'No, I'm sorry.'

'Well, you've been very helpful,' Millson told her. 'Thank you.'

As the door closed behind her, he turned to Scobie. 'The report of the interview with Vicki Calcot didn't mention her having an argument with Maisie. Send a WDC along to have another word with the girl and find out what they were arguing about.'

In the rear room of the antiques shop on the corner of the square and East Street, a woman detective-constable coaxed answers from a wide-eyed Vicki Calcot. Vicki was an elfin child, her shoulder-length brown hair tied back with blue ribbon. She sat on the couch beside her mother looking nervous. The policewoman, notebook in hand, sat on a stool in front of them.

'Maisie and me was talking about old Mother Hawksby,' Vicki explained to the policewoman.

'Vicki!' her mother said sharply.

'Sorry . . . *Madame* Hawksby.'

'What about her?' prompted the WDC.

'We didn't think she'd ever been a ballet dancer—not with her figure.'

'Maisie didn't mention she was meeting anyone, or anything like that?' asked the policewoman.

'No.'

'And you didn't notice anyone following the two of you?'

Vicki brushed her long dark hair off her forehead and screwed up her eyes.

'No.'

The WDC waited. When it was clear Vicki wasn't going to add anything she said, 'Someone who saw you outside the sweetshop together said you and Maisie were having an argument. What was it about?'

Vicki's eyes flashed in panic. The panic wasn't seen by her mother sitting beside her. Nor by the WDC bent over her notebook, forgetful of Chief Inspector Millson's maxim: 'Always watch their eyes when you ask a question.'

When Vicki didn't answer, the policewoman looked up. 'Well?'

Vicki's face was composed again. 'I wanted an ice-cream

and Maisie didn't, so she wouldn't come in the shop with me. That's all.'

No way was Vicki going to reveal the real reason Maisie wouldn't go into Nunn's with her. Not in front of her mum.

Millson and Scobie accepted the Baxters' hospitality for a second night and that evening, after dinner, they returned to the Incident Room to study the map display. Chalked on a board alongside it were figures, updated by a clerk at intervals—mainly for the benefit of the media—showing the number of people interviewed and the number of statements taken.

The map was now thick with coloured pins, each pin marking the reported or confirmed position of a person at the moment Maisie Brown was last seen. The display was developing like a polaroid film, more of the picture emerging all the time. It was a disappointment to Millson, though. In the cluster of pins around the Blood Alley area the red ones, indicating men, had all been accounted for. Among the pins further away were two grey ones, indicating their position was unconfirmed. The one in Chapel Street was Ronald Craig and the other, stuck into the quay, was Ernie Turner.

Millson stared gloomily at the display. For all the effort that had gone into making it, it brought him no nearer to finding Maisie Brown.

'You know what bugs me, Norris?' he said. 'How the hell did he take her through that crowd of people in her bright red outfit without being seen?'

In bed that night, Vicki Calcot lay fretting over the lie she'd told the policewoman. She just couldn't have told her what she and Maisie were actually arguing about. She hoped it didn't matter 'cos it was awful about Maisie being kidnapped.

Vicki chewed away at her nails, wishing she could talk to someone so she'd know if it really mattered or not.

TUESDAY

CHAPTER 7

The next morning, Tuesday, Carol Brown refused to be sedated further. She told the WPC who'd been stationed at her house to protect her from the media and freak phone calls, she wanted to make a television appeal for Maisie's safe return.

The WPC reported the request to the Incident Room and Millson sent a car to whisk Carol Brown up there before she could approach an ITN or BBC reporter direct. At the sight of the charts and diagrams in the operations room she burst into tears. Millson put his arm round her and steered her into his office.

Patiently he waited for her to recover, keeping firmly aloof from her distress. He wouldn't function effectively if he lost his detachment. As it was, Maisie's picture in Carol's sitting-room had brought a fleeting vision of Dena at that age and he'd felt a jolt of Carol Brown's pain like an electric shock.

He offered her a cigarette. She took one, clamping it between trembling lips.

He lit it for her and she said shakily, 'I'd almost given up smoking, you know. Now I can't stop.'

'Are you quite sure you want to make this appeal?'

'Yes. I must do *something* to help or I'll go mad.'

He nodded understandingly. An appeal by the mother of a missing child would be given full coverage. Shots of her distressed face on television screens would evoke a wide response. He needed publicity . . . to dredge up scraps of information . . . hopefully a clue. So far, despite the mass of information, he had nothing of use. And time was running out for Maisie Brown.

'Let me help you prepare what to say,' he said.

The press conference was held in front of the police trailer with Carol Brown sitting at a table and Millson and Scobie seated on either side of her.

'Don't worry,' Millson told her when she said she was afraid she'd break down and cry. 'They'll do additional takes if necessary.'

In the middle of her appeal she did break down . . . completely. The film crews, heavy video cameras perched on their shoulders, continued filming. Millson didn't stop them. Carol Brown was a heartrending sight and he knew from experience this would give the interview maximum impact. Let the newsrooms edit out footage of her distress if they wanted to. He doubted they would.

Carol managed to finish what she wanted to say and the cameras and microphones moved to Millson. He repeated his request for people in Tanniford on Saturday afternoon to come forward and for anyone with information to phone the Incident Room.

'No,' he admitted in answer to a question, 'the police have no leads at present.'

While the reporters were adding their own comments on camera, he escorted Carol Brown to the car. A reporter stepped forward and thrust a microphone at her.

'What are your feelings about this, Mrs Brown?'

Millson reached out and closed a hairy hand over the microphone. 'What d'you think they are?' he snapped. 'Sod off!' He thrust the microphone back in the man's face.

At her desk in the estate agency that morning, Kathy Benson dealt with the unopened correspondence left yesterday by Gerald Turner. She wondered if she should phone her parents about Maisie yet. They were on a three month tour of Australia and Carol had left the decision to her. If she told them, they'd abandon their holiday . . . fly straight back. And there was nothing they could do. Except worry. No, Kathy decided, leave them in peace for a while.

Her attention was caught by a movement outside. She thought it was someone perusing the advertisements of properties for sale until she noticed the small girl hovering at the window looking in. Her heart gave a leap and she jumped up. Then she saw it wasn't Maisie. It was her friend, Vicki Calcot.

Kathy went to the door and opened it. 'Do you want to see me, Vicki?'

Vicki nodded. She'd chewed all her nails off last night and this morning her mother kept carrying on at her about it and asking what was the matter. Vicki was desperate for someone to share her problem with and Maisie's auntie seemed the best person.

'You'd better come in then,' Kathy said.

She held the door wider. With a glance behind her as if someone might be watching, the child stepped inside. Kathy returned to her desk and sat down. Vicki stood in front of the desk, her eyes wandering over the photographs of houses on the wall behind Kathy.

'Is there something you want to ask me, Vicki?'

The child's eyes stopped wandering and focused on Kathy. She seemed unable to begin.

'It's all right, you can ask me anything you like,' Kathy said reassuringly. 'I won't mind what it is.'

Vicki's face brightened. 'There was summat I didn't tell the policelady . . . and I jus' wondered if it mattered . . . that's all.'

'Was it about Maisie?' Kathy asked quickly.

'Sort of.'

Kathy came from behind the desk and took hold of her by the shoulders. 'Vicki, this could be terribly important. Please tell me what it is.' She watched the girl waver and lower her head. On a sudden thought she added: 'I won't tell your mother.'

Vicki's head came up. 'Promise?'

'I promise.' She'd break the promise if she had to, to find Maisie. She pushed Vicki gently into a chair. 'Now . . . what is it you didn't tell the policewoman?'

'Well . . . she asked what me and Maisie was arguing about outside old Nunn's shop. I told her Maisie wouldn't come in with me 'cos she didn't want no ice-cream.' Vicki took a breath. 'Well, it weren't true.'

'I see,' Kathy said. 'So what was the truth?'

'I told Maisie how we could get a free one from old Nunn, but she wouldn't do it. *That's* what we was arguing about.'

Kathy frowned. 'I don't understand?'

'Well, what you do . . .' Vicki gave a nervous giggle and said in a rush, 'You hang about in the shop—bending over the freezer pretending to choose, see? Nunny comes up behind . . . puts his hand up your dress and says, "Help yourself, my dear, it's free." You grab one and run out quick.'

Kathy kept her voice level. 'And you did that on Saturday?'

'No—he wasn't there, was he? Out taking pictures, I 'spect.'

'What do you mean?'

'Well, I saw him with his video camera while we were marching. Kneeling he was, for a good view.' She giggled. 'I think he's a knicker-monster.'

Sidney Nunn's antics might be a giggle to Vicki. In Kathy they set alarm bells ringing. She warned Vicki to keep away from Nunn's shop and sent her home.

Then she reached for the phone.

'Looks like we have a child molester, Norris,' said Millson after Kathy's call. 'Man called Nunn in the newsagent's.

Question is, where was he at four o'clock Saturday? Have a look through the reports, will you?'

While Scobie was finding the report, Millson went into the Operations Room and studied the wall diagram of the Blood Alley area. There were two map pins in Nunn's the newsagent's: a red one for Nunn and a yellow one for his wife.

Scobie appeared with a DC's report in his hand. 'According to this,' he said, scanning it, 'Nunn went out to film the fête at three o'clock and returned at three forty-five. He then went into his stockroom to work and didn't come out again until about five o'clock. His wife confirms.' He looked up. 'That explains him not being in the shop when Vicki Calcot went in at four.'

Millson turned to the plan on the wall. 'The shop backs on to Baker's Passage. He could have slipped out without his wife knowing. It seems he was very interested in the majorettes—which means he probably knew exactly when Maisie Brown would be coming along that alleyway on her way home.'

Scobie said, 'And Holy Joe told us Nunn parked his van in Station Road on Saturday—near the end of Baker's Passage.'

Millson took a cigarette from the packet on the table and lit it. 'Here we have a man who likes fingering little girls. He goes down the quay to film the majorettes . . . comes back to his shop at quarter to four—yards from where Maisie Brown disappeared—and isn't seen again till five o'clock.'

He drew on his cigarette and blew out smoke. 'We need to see that video, Norris. You and a DC go talk to him. No mention of the little girl's accusation—understand? We can deal with that later, if need be. Tell him we've heard he took a video of the fête and we're collecting all the film and photos we can lay hands on. Mind, he won't cough it up easily—not if it contains the sort of material I think it does.

He'll try to delay so he can wipe it clean or edit it. *I want that tape, Norris.* Don't come back without it!'

Sidney Nunn was behind the counter when Scobie and a detective-constable entered his newsagent's. He wore an open-necked shirt and baggy trousers. Nunn was heavily built and about fifty with greying hair that had been turned glossy black by the application of a cosmetic colourant.

'Detective-Sergeant Scobie,' said Scobie, showing his warrant card. 'I think you know DC Jones. He interviewed you on Sunday. May we have a word?'

'Yes, come through to the office.' Nunn lifted a flap on the counter. They went through and followed him into a hallway. 'Maureen!' he shouted up the stairs. 'See to the shop for a moment.'

A small, plump woman with white hair came down the stairs, nodded to the two policemen and went into the shop.

Nunn took them into an office at the rear. There was a door out to the yard and through the window Scobie saw a gate into Baker's Passage beyond. Another door in the room, next to the one to the yard, had the word STOREROOM painted on it.

Nunn dropped into a swivel chair behind a table littered with invoices. Scobie carefully positioned a chair to the side of Nunn and sat down. DC Jones stationed himself in front of the storeroom door and remained standing.

'As you know, Mr Nunn,' Scobie said, 'we're appealing for information in connection with the disappearance of Maisie Brown.'

He nodded. 'Yes. Terrible business.'

'One of the things we're doing is to gather in any photos or film taken at the fête on Saturday. We understand you took some video film.'

'Ye-es.' Nunn's tone was suddenly cautious.

'We'd like to see it.'

'Oh, I don't think it would be of any help to you, Sergeant.'

'We don't know until we see it, do we?'

Nunn looked uncertain. After a moment he said, 'Actually, there was very little of interest on it and I've re-used the tape.'

'Pity,' Scobie said. He saw the relief in Nunn's face and knew he was lying. 'You didn't perhaps copy some of it to another tape?'

Nunn's eyelids flickered as though a pin had been stuck in him. 'No, I'm sorry,' he said, and Scobie suspected another lie.

During his visit on Sunday, as well as cartons of sweets and chocolates in the storeroom, DC Jones had noticed a video camera and a shelf of tapes. Scobie was banking on the camera not having been used since Saturday and the tape still being in it. He'd briefed Jones on what to do.

'There's a slight query following the last interview with you,' he told Nunn. 'Could the constable have another look in your storeroom?'

Nunn looked confused. 'I-er . . .'

Scobie gave a quick nod and Jones turned and was inside the storeroom door before Nunn realized what was happening. When Nunn jumped up he found his way blocked by six-foot Norris Scobie.

'It's all right, he doesn't need any help, Mr Nunn.'

Jones emerged with the video camera. He pressed a button and a tape cassette popped up.

'Here, leave that alone, it's mine!' Nunn tried to reach round Scobie for it.

'Easy . . . easy,' Scobie said soothingly. 'Have you used the camera since Saturday?'

'No . . . *yes!* I *told* you . . . I've re-used the tape,' he said aggressively. 'What's on there is private and you have no right to take it. Give it to me!' He struggled to reach the tape as Jones removed it from the camera.

Scobie held him back, wrinkling his nose in distaste at the smell of the man's hair oil. He said in a formal voice, 'From information received I have reason to believe this videotape contains pictures of a missing child. I am therefore taking it away for examination and you will be given a receipt for it.'

That stopped Nunn in his tracks, Scobie noted with satisfaction. He'd taken a strong dislike to the man.

'All right, take it,' Nunn muttered. 'There's no law against filming public events.'

'There is about withholding evidence though,' Scobie told him.

'I said you can take it,' Nunn said sourly, dropping back into his chair.

Better let them have it than search the storeroom and find the master tape he'd copied all the best bits on to. At least on the camera tape the footage of the majorettes contained crowd scenes as well.

Jones transferred the tape to his pocket and replaced the camera in the storeroom. Scobie tore a page from his pocketbook, scribbled a receipt and handed it to Nunn. Nunn dropped it on the table without looking at it.

'There's another matter I'd like to ask you about,' Scobie said.

'What's that?'

'Your van. A white Ford Escort, isn't it?'

'Yes.' Nunn's eyes slid sideways as DC Jones took out a notebook.

'A witness saw it parked in Station Road on Saturday afternoon.'

'I couldn't park in the High Street because of the procession.'

'Did you use the vehicle on Saturday?'

'Yes, to deliver video films. I order them from the distributors and deliver to hire shops around the county. The road was closed while the fête was on so I had to wait until the evening.'

'What time in the evening?'

'I don't see what that's got to do with anything.'

'We're interested in any vehicle that left Tanniford after four o'clock.'

'Oh, yes . . . I see.' Nunn's face twitched nervously. 'I left here at six.'

'Where did you go?'

'I can give you the addresses from my order book.'

He went into the storeroom and came out with a ledger. Turning the pages, he reeled off three addresses. Scobie made him repeat them slowly for Jones to write down. Then for each address, he asked Nunn his time of arrival and time of departure. Although Nunn was precise about leaving Tanniford at six and returning at nine, he was vague about the times in between. He hedged them with 'about' and 'could have been' and seemed unsure how long he'd spent at each address.

Scobie asked if these were the only places he'd been to that evening. Nunn said they were. He'd begun to sweat, droplets of perspiration appearing in the glossy black of his hair. And the underarms of his shirt were stained with damp.

'That's all for now then, Mr Nunn,' said Scobie.

Immediately after the two policemen left, Sidney Nunn phoned Charles Cresswell.

'The police have been here,' he said. 'I have to see you right away.'

CHAPTER 8

On his return to the Incident Room Scobie found Millson sitting with the operator at the computer terminal. He was studying the screen as the operator called up cases similar to Maisie Brown's from the PNC databank at Hendon.

Scobie tapped him on the shoulder. Millson turned, his face brightening as he saw the videotape in Scobie's hand.

'Good man.' Millson stood up. On the other side of the room Baxter was ticking off the names on the electoral roll of people who'd been interviewed. 'Baxter, you've got a video recorder, haven't you?'

'Yes, sir.'

'We'll need a cassette adaptor too,' Scobie said. 'This is a small camera tape.'

'No problem,' Baxter said.

'Right. Let's go see what we've got,' said Millson.

Sidney Nunn hurried along the narrow street at the side of the timber yard and in through the gates of Cresswell Marine. He was carrying a small suitcase.

Two months ago the boatyard would have been full of motor cruisers laid up for the winter. Now, the cruisers were out on hire and the yard was almost empty. Overhead the sun shone warmly and on the river a light breeze ruffled the surface of the water.

Sidney Nunn didn't appreciate the idyllic scene as he scampered across the yard on his way to Charles Cresswell's office. He was worried sick.

Mounting the external stairway, he entered the outer office on the first floor of the Cresswell Marine building. He paused, taken aback for a moment by the dark-haired girl sitting at a typewriter. He'd last seen Zena Baz through the lens of his camera on Saturday.

He hurried on to the door of Cresswell's room and went in. Cresswell sat at his mahogany desk wearing his customary navy blazer and the tie of the Royal Yachting Association.

'What's Zena Baz doing here?' Nunn asked.

'She's helping out. With Carol away over this Maisie affair, I need someone to handle the paperwork.'

Carol Brown had been Cresswell's secretary for four years. Her absence at this time of year—the peak period in his boat chartering business—was a serious handicap.

He eyed Nunn's suitcase. 'What's so urgent you had to rush down here right away?'

'I need your help, Charles. The police have been questioning me about Saturday evening.'

'Why?'

'They're checking on all vehicles that left Tanniford after Maisie Brown disappeared.'

'Well, I don't see what you're in a lather about. You were only delivering—' He stopped. 'You *were* delivering straight videos as well, weren't you?'

'Yes, of course. But the police will check the addresses and times.'

'So what? They'll do that with everyone won't they?' Cresswell asked.

'Charles, you don't understand. If they start working out journey times they'll find there's an hour of my time unaccounted for. The time I spent delivering to our own special customers.'

Cresswell fingered his chin. 'Ye-es. I see. They won't go to that trouble, though, will they?'

'I think they will. And I think they might pay me another visit . . . maybe search the place. That's why I want you to hide these tapes for me.' He lifted the suitcase onto Cresswell's desk.

'Cresswell raised his eyebrows. 'I thought you told me your place was clean?'

'It is . . . of our stuff. These are . . . well . . . my own personal tapes. I wouldn't want the police to get hold of these.'

'I see.' Cresswell leaned back in his chair with an amused smile. 'OK, stop worrying. I'll put them in the safe for you.'

The tape ran for thirty minutes. They watched it in silence on the television screen in Baxter's front room. The majorettes' display on the quay had been filmed in prurient detail. The zoom lens lingered in close-up on young faces and childish thighs, intermixed with low angle shots of lifting skirts.

At the end of the performance the camera followed the girls up the High Street and panned along the spectators lining the route. Abruptly, the picture left the screen as the tape came to an end and rewound itself.

Millson, who'd chain-smoked throughout the film, gazed at the blank screen, puffing and frowning. Nunn had filmed Maisie Brown. Obsessively . . . indecently. He'd filmed the other majorettes in the same way though, not just her. Millson shrugged his shoulders. 'So he's a peeper as well as a feeler,' he said. 'Doesn't help us much.'

'There's more, sir,' Scobie said. 'He drove out of Tanniford in his van at six o'clock and didn't get back till nine.'

Millson eyebrows lifted. 'Did he now? Where'd he go?'

'He gave three addresses. Says he was delivering videos. Vague about times, though. Another thing. There's a gate from his yard into Baker's Passage. It would be possible to slip out of the storeroom without his wife knowing. He could have nipped out to the alley, taken Maisie and put her in the van. Then driven off with her at six o'clock.'

Millson rubbed his chin. 'It's possible.' He turned to Baxter. 'What d'you know about this man Nunn?'

'He and his wife have lived here for years. They seem to have plenty of money. No kids. I've never heard anything against him. Always thought him respectable . . . till I saw this video.'

'What about impounding the van and letting forensic check it over?' Scobie suggested.

Millson shook his head. 'We haven't enough to justify that. And if this snatch was planned as carefully as I think it was, the child would have been encased in a dustbin bag. There wouldn't be a hair or fibre from her anywhere.' He came to his feet. 'Let's have those addresses visited and checked. I want to know the time he arrived at each of them and the time he left. When we've got those, we'll go over his route with him and see how his story stands up.'

He stubbed his cigarette in an ashtray and turned to Baxter again. 'Meantime, I want you to go through that tape carefully. It looks to have ended not long before Maisie and her friend walked down the High Street. There were people in the background of those last shots. Pick out the men and check them against the pins in our map. See if you can spot one who hasn't come forward yet.'

Charles Cresswell strolled across the boatyard, admiring the gleaming motor cruiser moored there. *Moonstreak* was the fleet leader, only hired to a select few. Frank Belmer, in white T-shirt and jeans, was refuelling her prior to putting her out on her mooring in the river. He lifted the nozzle of the fuel pipe from the cruiser's tank and replaced it in the pump.

'What did Nunn want?' he asked Cresswell. 'I saw him just now. He was hurrying like he'd shit himself.'

Charles Cresswell's mouth tightened in disapproval. Belmer was coarse, but he did his job of supervising the watermen and staff who serviced the fleet of cruisers well enough. The luxury cruisers of the Cresswell Marine fleet always went out on hire in spotless condition and with correct inventories.

'Mr Nunn was worried because the police have been questioning him about his movements on Saturday.'

'P'raps *he* snatched that kid, eh?' Belmer laughed unpleasantly.

'Don't be absurd!' At the back of Charles Cresswell's mind a memory stirred uneasily.

Belmer wiped his hands on a piece of rag. 'You haven't forgotten I'll be moving on soon?'

'No.' Cresswell shook his head.

Frank Belmer had turned up in Tanniford two months ago. It was just at the time Cresswell's fleet manager, John Harding, had suffered a heart attack and been ordered by his doctor to rest. Belmer had had experience at various marinas abroad and Cresswell had been only too glad to employ him, even lending him a furnished house in Ferry Street because he had nowhere to live.

Now, however, Harding was recovering. He would soon be fit for work again and Belmer's departure would suit Cresswell.

Returning to his office, he opened a drinks cabinet and poured himself a large whisky. He sank into an armchair, thinking about Sidney Nunn.

For two years he and Nunn had been making regular trips in *Moonstreak* across the North Sea to Amsterdam, using the North Sea Canal from Ijmuiden. Ostensibly, these were pleasure trips. Cresswell, however, was in partnership with a man in the *rossburt* district of Amsterdam called Van Beck. Van Beck supplied him with hard porn video films—the kind that risked instant seizure by customs, arrest and a term of imprisonment. They were high quality professional copies made from originals and fetched upwards of two hundred pounds each in the UK.

The videotapes, a hundred each trip, were concealed

behind the teak panelling in the cruiser's main cabin in case of a visit from customs on their return. Customs men seldom bothered with small pleasure craft, though, unless they received a tip-off.

It was a lucrative venture and Cresswell and Nunn were making a great deal of money out of it. Cresswell provided the vessel and the capital and Nunn handled the distribution. Supplying ordinary video films to hire shops gave Nunn cover for delivering 'specialist' ones to certain other customers.

The imported tapes were stored in a locked cupboard at Cresswell Marine. In his own storeroom, Nunn kept only the next batch due for delivery. Sunday, when the police first called to interview him and looked in his storeroom, had been a close shave.

Charles Cresswell leaned across to the cabinet and added another lump of ice to his drink. Frank Belmer's words, 'Perhaps *he* snatched that kid,' nagged at him. It was because of what had happened on the last trip to Amsterdam with Nunn.

They had called to see Van Beck and review the latest material as usual. Nunn was intrigued by one particular tape and asked Van Beck if that kind of gratification was available in Amsterdam.

The Dutchman laughed throatily. 'You like your fruit green—*onrijp, ya? Een jong meisje? Een kind?*' He laughed again and named a street behind the Oude Kerk. 'You could try there.'

Nunn was reluctant to wander around the *rossburt* alone and induced Cresswell to accompany him. They walked to the Voorburg Wal and sat on a concrete bench beside the canal. After they'd sat for some time in the evening gloom, a small shadow passed behind them. A few moments later it returned. This time she passed in front, glancing at them sideways. The dim light gave her ash-blonde hair a faint sheen. Cresswell heard Nunn catch his breath.

The girl stopped and stood looking over the low wall running along the canal. She was barely tall enough to see over it. Casually, Nunn rose to his feet and approached her. Cresswell heard the mumured conversation.

'Hallo, pet,' said Nunn.

She turned and looked up at him. '*Engels?*'

He nodded.

She spoke in English. 'You want nice time . . . play with me?'

'How much?' he asked.

'Three hundred guilder. You pay me now.'

Nunn took out his notecase, extracted the notes and held them out. In a blur of movement she snatched the money . . . turned . . . bolted.

'*Dank U wel.*' Her laughing child's voice floated back on the night air.

'Little bitch!' Angrily, Nunn returned to the seat.

'Serves you right,' Cresswell had told him.

Cresswell sipped his whisky, remembering Nunn's angry frustration. Was it possible he'd taken Maisie Brown? Driven her out of Tanniford in his van on Saturday night?

He chewed his lip. If Nunn was arrested, his own connection with him would come to light. He poured himself another whisky, a large one.

By half past two that afternoon, Ted Baxter and the map clerk had accounted for all the people in the background of Sidney Nunn's film except two. Baxter told Scobie he wasn't sure who they were, but he thought they were from the village.

'Kathy Benson probably knows them,' he said. 'Shall I get her up here?'

'Yes, OK. But make sure she only sees the crowd scenes. I don't want her upset by seeing those pictures of Maisie.'

*

The detectives visiting the addresses Sidney Nunn had delivered to on Saturday evening, returned at four o'clock. The addresses were video hire shops as Nunn had said. He'd spent only a few minutes at each. The DCs pointed out the locations to Millson and Scobie on a road map and gave their estimates of times and distances.

The furthest address was twenty miles away and by the most direct route along main roads the round trip came to sixty miles. Even driving at only thirty miles an hour, Nunn would have had nearly an hour to spare, allowing for stops.

Millson's eyes gleamed. 'Let's go ask him what he did with the extra time, Norris.'

Sidney Nunn tensed when he saw them entering the shop. Not only was the six foot Sergeant Scobie back, this time he had with him a fearsome-looking man with the body of a gorilla.

'Detective Chief Inspector Millson,' said the gorilla-shaped man. 'As the result of my sergeant's call this morning, I'd like to ask you some questions, Mr Nunn.' His mouth curved in a benign smile.

Nunn didn't know it, Scobie thought, but the smile was a bad sign. George Millson only smiled like that when he was about to skewer someone.

Nunn returned a half-hearted smile of his own. 'Come through to the office, Chief Inspector.'

He called his wife down to mind the shop again and took them into the rear room.

Millson took a road map from his briefcase and spread it on the table. 'I'd like you to look at this map and show us, please, the route you took on your journeys Saturday evening.'

Nunn remained calm. They would have already worked that out for themselves.

'Certainly, Chief Inspector.'

He bent over the map. Millson and Scobie watched him

trace a circular route from Tanniford covering the three destinations. It was the way they'd assumed he'd gone.

'Sure of that, are you?' Millson asked.

'Yes.'

'H'm.' Millson put a hand under his chin and rubbed it back and forth. 'That's a round trip of about sixty miles. Wouldn't take more'n a couple of hours. Spend some time at these places, did you? Chatting over business perhaps?'

Nunn smirked inwardly. He wasn't falling into that trap. They'd probably checked with the shops and discovered there was an hour to spare. He had an explanation worked out.

'No, I didn't hang about. I wanted to get back to watch a programme on telly.'

'And did you?' Millson's voice was casual, interested. 'Watch the programme, I mean?'

'No. Unfortunately, I broke down on the way back. The engine overheated . . . faulty waterpump, I think. The radiator boiled and I had to stop and wait for it to cool down. Then I filled up with water and drove slowly home.'

'Uh-huh. Went to a garage for the water, did you?'

'No. I always carry a jerrycan of water in the van. I've had the trouble before. I can show you the can if you like,' Nunn said earnestly. Too earnestly in Scobie's view. Nunn seemed over-anxious to be believed.

'I'd rather you showed me where you had this breakdown,' Millson said.

Nunn bent over the map. It had better be after his last call, else they'd wonder why he hadn't mentioned the breakdown to the next shop he called at. He visualized the road, choosing a likely spot.

'There,' he said, putting a finger on the map. It was where he knew there was a lay-by.

Millson peered at where he was pointing. 'You stopped there?'

Nunn nodded. 'For about an hour.'

'An hour?' Millson's eyebrows lifted sceptically.

'It takes a long time for a car radiator to cool down. You can't put cold water—'

Millson cut him short. 'What time was this?'

'Oh-er . . .' Nunn hesitated, desperately trying to work out distances and times. Safest to deduct an hour from the time he got back. 'About eight o'clock,' he said recklessly.

Even before Millson pounced, he realized his mistake. Millson stabbed the map with his finger. 'That place is all of twenty miles away. If you had waited there for an hour you couldn't possibly drive to Tanniford by nine—even at the speed of Concorde.'

Nunn stared at the map again as though mesmerized. At last he said, 'Perhaps it was less than an hour . . . maybe it was only half an hour.' It was weak, but it was the best he could think of. 'I wasn't watching the time.'

Scobie looked up from taking notes. 'I thought you said you were anxious to get back to watch telly?'

With an effort Nunn kept his voice from shaking. 'Well, yes, but I didn't keep looking at my watch. Anyway, I'm not sure I was back as early as nine,' he added lamely.

'If you weren't, it would mean you took even longer to cover those sixty miles,' Scobie said.

Nunn saw Millson staring at him unnervingly. Millson was considering whether to impound Nunn's van after all. A motor engineer should be able to disprove the overheating story and a forensic examination might link the van to Maisie Brown. He decided he still didn't have enough justification.

'The sergeant will take a statement from you, Mr Nunn. We'll continue with this tomorrow.'

Sidney Nunn nodded, his face expressionless.

In Tanniford that evening the man sat watching the latest report about Maisie Brown in the television news. Carol Brown's tearful face appeared on the screen as she made her appeal for Maisie's safe return. He leaned forward to watch more closely. As Carol broke down, barely able to finish, he was filled with exhilaration. This had been an unexpected bonus.

At the end he sat back with a satisfied smile. The police hadn't a clue, not a bloody clue.

WEDNESDAY

CHAPTER 9

Sidney Nunn kept his face blank as Millson and Scobie came into his shop again Wednesday morning. Millson had decided to put Nunn's story of a breakdown to the test.

'We'll drive over the route with him, Norris. Breathe down his neck. Show him we don't believe his story,' he told Scobie.

'I'm not satisfied with the statement you made yesterday evening, Mr Nunn,' Millson said.

Nunn asked cautiously, 'What's wrong with it?'

'The explanation of your journeys Saturday evening for one thing. I find it hard to accept. I'd like us to drive over the route together and see how the times fit together.'

'Why? I don't see why it matters,' Nunn said stubbornly. 'You've no reason to connect me with the abduction of that child.'

'It's a matter of eliminating you from our inquiries,' Millson said smoothly. 'And we can't eliminate you until we resolve the problem of these journey times.'

'But what will my wife think? This is the fourth time I've had police here and this time you want me to go off in a car with you.' Nunn hoped he'd shown the right degree of impatience.

'We shan't be long. My car's outside,' Millson said unhelpfully.

Sidney Nunn was confident at the start of the journey. He'd taken the precaution of loosening one of the clips on the radiator hose of the van to allow it to leak a little. And he'd worked out an amended schedule that fitted in better with a breakdown. By shaving the time here, adding minutes there, he'd been able to make the story more credible. They might still not believe him, but there wasn't much they could do if he stuck to the story and kept his nerve. He was safe from a search now he'd moved the rest of his tapes to Cresswell's safe.

By the end of the drive he was less confident. Between them they'd put him through the wringer, jumping on every deviation from his original story and cross-examining him on it. At the lay-by where he said he waited for the engine to cool down, he was made to indicate the exact spot where he was supposed to have parked.

Scobie left the car and inspected the ground. 'Any other vehicle in the lay-by while you were here?'

'No.' It was the only safe answer.

The questioning continued remorselessly. When they let him out of the car back in Tanniford, Sidney Nunn was sweating like a racehorse at the finishing post.

In Millson's office he and Scobie munched the sandwiches Mrs Baxter had sent in, washing them down with beer sent up from the Falcon.

'We've no real evidence against him, Norris.' Millson poured beer into his glass.

'Surely we have? There's the tape with Maisie on it and he was within spitting distance of where she was snatched at four o'clock. He leaves Tanniford in his van as soon as the fête's over and there's a large chunk of his time unaccounted for.'

'It's all suspicion, Norris. Yes, he shows a perverted interest in majorettes, he had the opportunity and there's time unaccounted for. But none of it is evidence he actually abducted her.'

Millson bit moodily into another sandwich.

*

In her flat above the estate agent's, Kathy Benson too was having a snack lunch.

She poured a cup of coffee and picked up the local paper. It was a weekly paper, delivered that morning and there were pictures of Saturday's fête on the front page. There was no mention of Maisie Brown's disappearance, though. The paper had gone to press before the story broke.

Four days now, Maisie had been missing. Kathy drank her coffee, feeling dispirited. Carol had relapsed, disheartened yesterday morning's appeal had brought no news of her. Kathy had run out of ways to keep her sister's hopes alive. Ronald Craig was no help. He avoided being at home with Carol and spent his evenings drinking in the Station Arms, indifferent to her suffering.

Kathy glanced idly at the paper, scanning the photographs of the fête on the front page. Trudy Wilson was prominent, showing a great deal of leg. Another picture showed the line-up at the start of the Pram Race.

Kathy turned the page and cast a professional eye over the houses for sale. Suddenly she turned back to the front page and ran her eye along the line of contestants in the Pram Race. Her mind's eye switched to the section of Sidney Nunn's video Ted Baxter had asked her to look at yesterday afternoon. As he displayed the frames one at a time, she'd put names to the people he didn't know.

Her brows came together in a frown. She thought for a moment. Then she ran to her telephone and rang the Incident Room.

'I'd like to speak to Sergeant Scobie,' she said. 'It's very urgent.'

Scobie finished his lunch and joined the collators to sift through the latest reports.

George Millson swallowed the rest of his beer and lit a cigarette, reviewing possible suspects. Ernie Turner. He was sure Gerald Turner had been lying about his father's suicide. Craig. He wasn't easy about Maisie's stepfather, not all all easy. Sidney Nunn was his favoured suspect. An obvious motive . . . clear opportunity . . . and the van to take her away in. The type too, no doubting that.

Millson cupped his eyeballs in the palm of his hands and massaged them wearily. He needed time away from Tanniford. Time to view things from a distance and re-charge his batteries. He opened his door and called across to Scobie.

'Anything new?'

Scobie shook his head.

'We'll give the Baxters a break and go back to our own beds tonight,' Millson said.

Scobie gave him a thumbs up sign. He'd be glad to return to his flat. The three nights with the Baxters had been pleasant and Barbara Baxter fed them well. But sleeping in the same room as George Millson was purgatory. He chuntered around all night like a cement mixer, endlessly twisting and turning. Worst of all, he snored. Loudly. Scobie wondered if snoring had been an unspoken cause of Mrs Millson's departure.

A phone rang on the desk next to him. 'It's for you,' the WDC who answered told him. 'A Miss Benson.' She passed him the handset.

'I want to see the video again,' Kathy said.

'What for?'

'I'll tell you that when I've looked at it,' she said.

'OK. If you like to come up to Baxter's house we'll have it ready for you.'

Kathy came into Baxter's front room wearing a summer dress. The shade of blue set off her auburn hair to perfection, Scobie thought, as she sat down in front of the television.

'Which part d'you want to see again?' Baxter asked.

'I'd like to see the whole thing. From beginning to end,' she said.

Scobie started to say, tactfully, why he didn't think it was a good idea. Nunn had taken shots of Maisie that would upset her, he explained.

She brushed his protest aside. 'I'm a big girl.'

'OK, then.' He nodded to Baxter. 'From the beginning.' He sat down beside Kathy.

As he'd expected, she went rigid at sight of the majorettes. The film seemed even more salacious, watching it with Kathy. When Maisie appeared in close-up on the screen, Kathy reached out and gripped his hand. He was pleased when she leaned closer and kept on holding it.

She continued watching, grim-faced. 'Dirty old man,' she said at one point.

She said nothing more until near the end. As the camera moved in a panoramic sweep of the spectators by the railway bridge, she cried out, 'Stop! There . . . that's what I wanted to see. Give me the control.'

Baxter handed her the remote control. She backtracked, played forward again . . . and pressed the 'pause' button. The picture froze on a group of spectators.

She went to the screen and stooped down to examine the picture closely. 'I thought so.' She pointed to a figure in the crowd.

Scobie leaned forward. 'It's a woman with a pram.'

'No, it isn't. Look closer.'

He and Baxter stood up and bent to peer at the screen. It was Baxter who understood first. 'It's a man,' he said. 'It's one of the nannies in the Pram Race.'

'That's just the point.' Kathy opened the local newspaper she'd brought with her and showed them the front page. 'He *wasn't* in the Pram Race. Look at this photograph of the competitors. He's not there.'

Scobie took the paper from her and studied the picture. None of the nannies in the line-up looked like the one on the television screen.

'Perhaps his partner dropped out . . . or he changed his mind.'

'He didn't,' Kathy said. 'He didn't even enter. I checked with Charles Cresswell. He organizes the race and competitors have to register with him the day before. All the ones who did, took part.'

Scobie's thoughts surged ahead, possibilities tumbling over one another. 'Oh, Christ!' he breathed. 'Suppose—' He broke off. 'I'll get Mr Millson.'

He hurried out and down Baxter's drive to the police trailer.

Millson, enveloped in a cloud of smoke, looked up morosely as Scobie burst in on him. 'Where's the fire?'

Scobie resisted the temptation to say, 'In here by the look of it.' He recovered his breath and said, 'You remember you said Maisie Brown wouldn't have been abducted by a woman?'

'Yes, what of it?' Millson asked wearily.

'How about a woman who's really a man dressed as a woman?'

Millson eyed him balefully. 'What the hell are you blathering about?'

'Kathy Benson has spotted something on Nunn's video. You'd better come and look at it.'

Millson followed him into the house. He nodded to Kathy and moved an upright chair close to the television. Reversing it, he sat on it the wrong way round with his hands resting on the back.

'All right. Let's see whatever it is,' he snapped at Baxter.

Baxter ran the tape and froze the picture at the same point as Kathy had done. Scobie stood by the television screen and pointed to the figure in the crowd.

Millson leaned forward and lowered his chin on to his hands. 'It's a woman with a pram,' he said.

'When have you seen a woman wearing a hat like that?' Scobie asked smugly. 'And take a look at the pram.'

'OK,' Millson said patiently, 'so it's a man dressed as a nanny and he's waiting to take part in the Pram Race.'

Somewhat deflated by his quick appreciation, Scobie said, 'He didn't. Take part in the race, I mean. He wasn't even entered for it. There's a photo of the competitors in the local paper.' He held it out.

Millson's head reared up. He snatched the paper from Scobie and stared at the picture. He looked again at the television screen and swore softly under his breath. A *pram. A large Victorian pram.* A pram you could put a child in . . . covered up . . . hiding that conspicuous scarlet outfit. Wheel her away through the crowd . . . just another nanny with an old pram . . .

He raised his bulk awkwardly from the chair and stood up. Only Norris Scobie knew, by the look in his eyes, that George Millson's brain was in overdrive.

'Get my car, Norris. We're going to county headquarters. They've got some special equipment that performs miracles with video pictures.' At the door, he turned. 'You too, Miss Benson.'

It was a command, not an invitation.

The first action of the specialist film unit at county headquarters was to copy the tape. Then an operator loaded the copy tape into the display monitor and ran the film. The picture was clearer and larger than on Baxter's television.

'D'you want to see all of it, sir?' the operator asked Millson.

'No, only a bit near the end.'

The operator fast-forwarded the tape until Millson said, 'Just after this,' then ran it at half-speed and finally frame by frame. Millson tapped him on the shoulder and pointed to a figure with a pram among the crowd.

The operator moved a cursor across the screen. He pressed a key on his keyboard and the figure was highlighted in a circle of paler colour.

'Is it her you're interested in?'

Millson nodded.

'Let's see what computer enhancement can do then.' The man's fingers pecked at the keyboard. The figure grew larger and the features became more definite.

'How's that?'

'That's fine.' Millson stared at the screen and motioned Kathy forward. 'Recognize him?'

She put her head to one side and studied the figure carefully. After a while she shook her head. 'I'm afraid not. You can't see much of the face under that bonnet and with the wig and make-up . . . it could be anybody.'

'What about the clothes?'

'The clothes?' Kathy peered at them and frowned. 'It's a professional-looking outfit.'

'Meaning?'

'He didn't pick it up in some second-hand clothes shop. Look at the hat. That's a genuine poke bonnet.'

'A *what*?' Millson asked.

Kathy smiled. 'It's a type of Victorian hat—sometimes called a coal-scuttle bonnet because of the shape. It almost completely hides the face. I wonder where—' She stopped and moved closer to the screen.

'Yes?' Millson urged.

She said doubtfully, 'I think there are clothes like that in the Tanniford Drama Society's wardrobe. You'd have to ask Miss Humm—she's the wardrobe mistress—but I believe they used a bonnet like that in one of their productions.'

'Where is it—this wardrobe?'

'In the village hall.'

'Uh-huh.' Millson pointed to the picture again. 'And what about the pram?'

Kathy shrugged. 'Large Victorian four-wheeler. Difficult to come by these days.'

'Right.' Millson turned to the operator. 'Can you print me a copy of that picture—just as it is?'

'No problem.'

'And I shall want at least fifty copies for the teams.'

'Ah . . . now that *is* a problem. It's a slow process, you see. Not before morning, I'm afraid.'

Millson sighed. 'All right, morning it is.'

'Do you think this was the man who took Maisie?' Kathy asked as they left the building.

'It's possible. One thing's for sure, we need to identify him. Tomorrow we'll call on every house in Tanniford with the picture. There must be several people who saw him with that pram.'

In the car park Millson told Scobie, 'Take Miss Benson back to Tanniford in my car, Norris. You can drop me off at my place on the way and pick me up in the morning.' He turned to Kathy. 'Please don't mention this to anyone for the moment, Miss Benson—not even your sister.'

As Scobie turned the Sierra round outside Millson's semi-detached, Kathy stared at the peeling paint and overgrown garden. 'Is Chief Inspector Millson married?'

'Divorced,' Scobie said. 'The wife remarried and his daughter lives with her and the stepfather. I think George only keeps the house on because he hopes his daughter will come back to him one day.'

'How sad to wait for someone who never comes.'

It was more than sad, Scobie thought. It was eating away George Millson's heart.

'Do you think he was pleased with my help?' Kathy asked. 'He didn't say so.'

'Mr Millson never shows when he's pleased,' Scobie told her. 'He just looks a little less angry. That's when you know he's pleased.'

'It *was* important though, wasn't it?'

'Very. This could be a breakthrough. And . . .'

There was more chance of Maisie being alive. A man wouldn't take all that trouble if he was going to kill her straight away. That raised other dreadful possibilities though and Scobie didn't want to start Kathy thinking about those.

'I believe there's more hope,' he said.

She turned her head to look at him. 'You really think so?'

'Yes, I do.'

He drove for a while in silence. They were out in the country now and it was growing dark. He stole a sideways glance at her. In the glow of the dashboard Kathy Benson's face was soft and relaxed.

He said quietly, 'Mr Craig told us you had an affair with your sister's husband.' It was against the rules to disclose what another witness had said without a reason, but he wanted to see her reaction.

The muscles of her face tensed. 'It's not true. I wouldn't be so mean.'

'You were in love with him, though?'

She looked away from him, out of the window. 'Yes, very much.'

Remembering her tragic expression at the graveside and driven by some inner need to know, Scobie pressed on recklessly. 'And you're still carrying the torch for him.'

Her head whipped round and she said sharply, 'Don't be ridiculous! He's dead. Anyway, it's none of your business.'

There was silence between them for the rest of the journey.

As Scobie brought the car to a halt outside her flat in Tanniford she asked him, 'Would you like to come in for a coffee?'

'No, thank you.'

She half opened the door then paused. 'Look . . . I was rude to you and I'm sorry. It's a long drive back. Please come in for a moment.'

Scobie felt her hand lightly touch his arm. He turned his

head. Her eyes were hollows of darkness in the pale face, her lips slightly parted. She looked ethereal . . . beautiful.

He said quickly, 'OK then, thanks.'

The entrance to her flat above the estate agency was in Baker's Passage at the rear of the premises. Opening the gate, Kathy looked along the passage into the yawning darkness. Down there, some monster had lain in wait for little Maisie and . . . Kathy shivered. Scobie slipped his arm round her. He kept it there as they ascended the iron staircase to the flat above.

'You haven't had anything to eat, have you?' Kathy said, as she filled the electric kettle.

'No. I can get something in Tanniford though, I expect.'

She laughed. 'Not a chance! There's only the fish and chip shop and the Old Bakehouse and they're both closed now.' She opened the fridge. 'Take a seat. It's just as easy to prepare for two as for one.'

'I won't argue with that,' Scobie said cheerfully.

He watched her put a carton into the microwave oven. 'Those things are a mystery to me. I guess I should learn to use one.'

'Don't you have a girlfriend to cook for you?'

He shook his head. 'It's mostly snack bars or the police canteen for me. My last girlfriend couldn't put up with the irregular hours. She married a civil servant.'

Kathy laughed. 'About Alec and me . . .' she began.

'You don't have to explain,' he said quickly.

'Yes, I do,' she said firmly. 'I want to. I fell in love with Alec a long time ago, before Maisie was born. I would have married him—' She stopped and gave a half-smile. 'Only Carol got him first.'

By tricking Alec into making her pregnant. For a moment the old hurt flared up again.

'The marriage didn't work out,' she went on. 'Alec tried to make it work for Maisie's sake, but he couldn't. In the end he asked Carol for a divorce so he could marry me.'

Her head drooped. 'That was just before his last trip. He never came back.'

She raised her head again and the violet eyes gazed steadily at Scobie. 'But there was no affair between us. I couldn't have done that . . . not to my own sister.'

In the churchyard opposite, a figure emerged from the shadows of the holly tree and followed the brick wall running along the back gardens of the houses in Ferry Street. It crossed the tarmac path that led from East Street entrance to the High Street and stole along the side of the church, past the church door and round to the door at the foot of the church tower.

After their meal Kathy took Scobie into the front sitting-room for coffee and realized she'd forgotten to close the curtains. She went to the window and as she drew the curtains, she looked out at the church. A flicker of light caught her eye. Pulling the curtain aside, she stared into the darkness.

'The church is on fire!' She ran to the telephone in the kitchen.

Scobie went to the window and looked out. Smoke and flames were coming from a window at the top of the church tower. He turned and made for the door. Kathy joined him from the kitchen.

'I've called the fire brigade,' she said. 'We must warn the Vicar.'

As they hurried down the steps from the flat a loud wailing sound broke the night air.

'What on earth's that?' Scobie asked.

'An air raid siren. It's to call out the firemen.'

They crossed the road and entered the churchyard, making for the vicarage behind the Falcon. Scobie pounded on the door until a bewildered-looking Mr Smollett emerged.

'Oh dear . . . oh dear,' he kept saying as Scobie explained there was a fire in the church tower.

Tanniford had its own fire engine. The fire station was next to the shipyard and manned part-time. As the Vicar hurried across the churchyard with Kathy and Scobie, a strident '*Ee-aw . . . ee-aw*' started up on the far side of the village as the fire engine roared out of its garage. Siren howling, it sped along Spring Street into East Street and thundered up the High Street to the churchyard gates. Two firemen in yellow helmets jumped down and began reeling out hose. Two others ran to a hydrant in the road and connected the other end.

'Oh, do be careful where you squirt water,' the Vicar wailed as the two firemen with the hose raced towards the door to the tower.

'Don't you worry none, Vicar,' one of them shouted, 'we'll soon have it under control.' They yanked open the door and pounded up the stone staircase inside.

The fire was soon out. The Leading Fireman came down from the tower and pushed his way through the crowd that had now gathered, to where the Vicar was standing with Kathy and Scobie.

Keeping his voice low, he said, 'I reckon fire was started deliberate, Vicar. We'll have to call the police.'

Scobie stepped forward. 'I'm a police officer . . . Detective-Sergeant Scobie.'

'You'd best come up the tower and take a look, then,' said the fireman.

Scobie followed him as he clumped up the stone steps in his heavy boots. The steps ended in a chamber at the top of the tower where a double trapdoor in the ceiling gave access to the flat roof. The fire had destroyed the wooden stairs that led up to the trapdoor and some of the flooring around them.

The fireman bent and picked up a piece of burnt wood with his gloved hand. He held it under Scobie's nose.

Scobie sniffed and nodded. 'Petrol.'

He returned down the steps to the churchyard and drew the Vicar and Kathy aside from the onlookers.

'The fireman's right, Mr Smollett. The fire was started deliberately.'

'Oh dear, this is dreadful . . . simply dreadful. Nothing like this has ever happened to me.' Vernon Smollett was wringing his hands. 'And I was so happy we'd collected enough money at the fête to begin the repairs to the tower.'

'There hasn't been much damage—except to the wooden steps to the roof. They've been completely destroyed.'

The Vicar's face brightened. 'Oh, that's not so bad.'

'Why would anyone start a fire up there?' Kathy asked.

'Who knows?' Scobie shrugged his shoulders. 'Maybe the forensic people will have some ideas. Meantime, perhaps you'd be good enough to see the building is securely locked, Mr Smollett.'

'Yes, very well. Oh dear . . . we've always been proud of not having to lock our church.'

Later, when Kathy said goodbye to him at the door of her flat, Scobie thought she leaned towards him. He took a chance, bent his head and kissd her on the lips. She didn't resist, so he pulled her closer and kissed her again. Her mouth was soft and yielding and the second kiss went on for a long time.

When he released her she was smiling. Her eyes seemed sad, though. Norris Scobie had the gloomy thought they'd never light up with happiness unless Maisie Brown was found alive and well.

Yesterday's appeal by Carol Brown was repeated on the evening television news. This time the man recorded it on the video. Now he could watch it whenever he liked.

There was an additional item—a policewoman holding up a red dress same as the kid was wearing. His mouth opened in a mirthless smile. She wasn't wearing it now.

THURSDAY

CHAPTER 10

In the small hours of Thursday morning Gerald Turner awoke from one of the nightmare dreams he'd been having since his father's suicide. He lay awake in bed, haunted by memories. The memory of his mother's ravaged face in those last weeks as the cancer destroyed her . . . a face so beautiful a few short months before. The memory of his father's death leap. And that terrible letter.

As a boy, it had always been a puzzle to Gerald why an attractive young woman like his mother had married his elderly, balding father. When he was thirteen, he asked her.

'He wasn't bald when I married him,' Rachel laughed. 'Why did I marry him? Well . . . he was kind to me . . . very kind. And I liked him . . . I still do. And . . .' She gave him an arch look. 'I was pregnant with you. I needed a husband.'

'You mean he's not really my father?'

She hesitated. 'Quite honestly, darling, I'm not really sure. He certainly could be. And the other candidate vanished with the speed of light when he heard I was preggers.'

'I don't like the thought of you . . .' Gerald's voice was strained. 'You and him . . . if he's not my father . . .'

'You mustn't be jealous, you silly boy. There's nothing to be jealous of.' She put her arms round him and kissed him on the mouth.

Rachel Turner had longed for a baby daughter. When Gerald was born she satisfied her yearning by dressing him in girl's clothes. She continued to do so until he was four and even then, for years after, he wore girls' underwear and went to bed in a nightdress.

There were no girls at the secondary school Gerald attended. The school governors had fought off combining with a girls' school during successive upheavals in the education system. The absence of girls meant that in school plays female characters had to be played by boys. Gerald Turner, with his feminine looks and slim build, was always one of the boys chosen for a female role. He didn't mind. He loved acting and he wasn't embarrassed at playing a female.

Shortly after his fourteenth birthday he played Juliet in the school's production of *Romeo and Juliet*. It was a turning point for Gerald. He discovered he not only loved acting—he loved dressing up as a girl.

The pleasure of wearing female apparel soon turned into a fixation. He started dressing in his mother's clothes and parading about in them when he was alone in the house.

One day Rachel came home unexpectedly and found him in her bedroom wearing one of her outfits. Gerald began stammering excuses.

'It's all right, darling,' she said. 'I don't mind you wearing my clothes if you want to.' She eyed him critically. 'Actually, they fit you rather well.'

He looked at her in astonishment. 'You really don't mind?'

'Of course not. I know how much you like it.'

'You mean you *knew*?' Relief flooded over him.

'Of course, darling.' Rachel stepped forward and ruffled his hair. 'We won't tell your father, though. He wouldn't understand.'

George Millson was in a relaxed mood when Scobie called for him that morning. An evening of quiet reflection with a whisky bottle had helped. So too had the interruption half way through the evening. A phone call from his daughter, Dena.

Dena had said she wanted to spend some of her summer holiday with him. 'Mummy's being difficult, but I've told her I'm old enough to decide for myself. We're still arguing about it.'

So there was hope, Millson decided and returned to the latest development on Maisie Brown in an optimistic frame of mind.

The more he thought about the man with the pram the more he became convinced he was the man who'd taken her. It couldn't be Sidney Nunn, because he took the film. Millson was still suspicious about those journeys Saturday evening, though. He didn't cross Nunn off his list of suspects, merely moved him lower down.

Ronald Craig? Millson couldn't see him bothering to dress up. And he wasn't the planning type. A man with his temper would have waited in the house and grabbed Maisie when she came home.

Ernie Turner remained a possibility. He could have returned to his house—his son was at the hospital—dressed up as a nanny and met Maisie in Blood Alley. Maisie would have gone off with him willingly. She'd have thought being hidden in the pram was a game. Yes, Ernie Turner could have taken Maisie. Then killed himself in a fit of remorse.

'Did you collect the pictures?' Millson asked Scobie as he heaved himself into the car.

'Yep and I've phoned Gladys Humm—she works in Tanniford Post Office. I've asked her to meet us at the village hall. I thought you'd probably want to ask her about the clothes before briefing the inquiry teams.'

'Good.' Millson nodded contentedly. 'There are mornings when I enjoy getting up, Norris, and there are mornings when I don't. This is one I do.'

Scobie glanced at him. It would take more than a new

development in the case to give George Millson's face that happy expression. 'Some good news, George?'

Millson nodded. 'My daughter wants to stay with me for a while . . . if her mother will let her.'

Scobie had never met George Millson's ex-wife, but from what little he said about her, Scobie had the impression she was a resentful woman. If George's happiness depended on her cooperation Scobie didn't hold out much hope for him.

On the drive to Tanniford, he told Millson about the fire in the church tower.

'We can do without distractions like that,' Millson said. He sighed. 'A kidnapping . . . a suicide . . . and now arson. I thought Baxter told us Tanniford was a quiet little backwater?'

Gerald Turner was fifteen when he met Charles Cresswell. It was when the Tanniford Amateur Dramatic Society put on *First a Girl* at the village hall. The script required the female lead to spend most of the play pretending to be a boy and the producer had been unable to find a suitable girl to play the part.

The producer happened to be the English master at Gerald's school. He decided to cast a boy in the role instead . . . a boy who could play a girl pretending to be a boy. Gerald Turner's performance as Juliet . . . his naturalness as a young girl . . . had impressed him. He offered him the part in *First a Girl* and Gerald jumped at it.

First a Girl was a great success and packed the village hall to capacity. On the last night Charles Cresswell, the chairman of the Dramatic Society, threw a party for the cast at his house in Tanniford Cross. They were whisked there in a minibus after the final curtain, still in their costumes.

At the party Gerald was thoroughly at ease behind his glamorous make-up. He was wearing a blue taffeta dress and his dark curls had been specially coiffured for the part by Beryl's Hair Salon. As he stood sipping champagne—something he'd never tasted before—he was approached by Charles Cresswell.

'A marvellous performance. You were wonderful—simply wonderful.' Beneath the distinguished grey hair, Cresswell's blue eyes appraised him.

'Thank you, kind sir.'

Reacting in character, Gerald smiled and fluttered his eyelashes. A young girl flattered by the attention of a handsome-looking man. After all, Charles Cresswell was an influential figure in the dramatic society.

At the end of the evening, as the other members of the cast started to leave, Gerald found Charles Cresswell at his side again.

'I'll drive you home,' he murmured.

On the way to Tanniford, heady with wine and half asleep, Gerald hardly noticed when the car turned off the road into Tanniford Woods. It came quietly to a halt and Cresswell switched off the engine.

In the shadowed interior of the car, faint moonlight through the windscreen reflected Gerald's pale face. Cresswell's eyes dwelt on the long eyelashes, smooth cheeks . . . soft red lips. With a strangled sob, he leaned across and kissed Gerald full on the mouth.

For a few seconds there was no resistance. Then the boy reared away with a gasp. 'What are you doing?'

Cresswell's hand reached down and gripped him through the dress. 'Come on . . . you know you want to.'

Tanniford's village hall was fifty yards up the hill from Ted Baxter's house, on the opposite side of the road from the Post Office. Gladys Humm was waiting for them in the entrance porch. She wore the same grey cardigan and skirt she'd been wearing at Monday's interview.

Millson greeted her. 'Good morning, Miss Humm. I

understand you look after the costume wardrobe for the dramatic society.'

'Oh yes, and I take part in their productions too, Chief Inspector.' Proudly, she pointed to a poster on the wall advertising a past performance of *Blithe Spirit*. 'I played Madame Arcati.'

Millson nodded politely. 'Any idea who's playing this character, Miss Humm?' He thrust a copy of the video picture at her. 'That was taken at the top of the High Street on Saturday.'

She tilted her head and studied the picture through the lower half of her bifocals.

'No, I'm afraid not. Those clothes look like the ones missing from our wardrobe, though.'

'These garments were stolen?'

Miss Humm's eyes flinched. 'Not necessarily stolen,' she said firmly. 'We always have one or two items missing by the end of the season. Sometimes people take their costumes home and forget to return them, you know. When I did an inventory check last week there were several items missing—including a bonnet like that man's wearing.'

'Why didn't you mention this when you saw me before?' Millson asked sharply.

Miss Humm's face turned deep red. 'You were very busy with the kidnap . . . and I didn't think it was important. Oh dear . . . is it?' She looked distressed.

'Maybe.' Millson patted her arm reassuringly. 'It's all right, Miss Humm. You had no way of knowing. Now, would you show us where you keep these costumes, please?'

'Yes, of course.' She took a bunch of keys from her handbag and unlocked the double doors to the entrancc.

Scobie noted the single action Yale. 'Who else has access to the building?' he asked as they followed her across the foyer and into the hall.

'Oh, lots of people. The Scouts . . . Guides . . . Women's

Institute . . . They all use the hall for meetings.' Miss Humm bustled to the stage at one end of the hall.

She led them through a door at the side of the stage and along a corridor beyond to a door marked 'Wardrobe'. Selecting a key from her bunch, she unlocked it. There was a smell of greasepaint and powder as she opened the door and they stepped inside. Around the room there were rails of garments on hangers and on shelves along the wall, boots and shoes and various forms of headgear.

'We hire the costumes for most of our productions,' Miss Humm explained. 'But we also have quite a collection of our own which we use for Christmas pantomimes and variety shows.'

Millson glanced along the shelf of hats. 'Is this where that bonnet should be?'

'Yes. And I think the skirt was one of these.' Miss Humm pushed apart the hangers on a rail to reveal some navy blue skirts. 'We use these for policewoman and schoolmistress characters. The skirt that's missing is one of the outsize ones we keep for the larger ladies of our company.' She turned. 'And there are three wigs missing from the cupboard over there.'

'*Three* wigs?' Scobie queried.

Miss Humm said patiently, 'That's not unusual, Sergeant. They'll probably reappear next season.'

'I doubt if the one *he's* wearing will,' Millson said, tapping the picture in his hand, 'or the clothes. Tell me, how many men belong to this amateur dramatics thing?'

'If you mean the Tanniford Players,' she said primly, 'there are six regular actors. However, when we put on musicals and pantomimes all sorts of people join in. We have plenty of talent in Tanniford.'

'Any female impersonators among them?' Scobie asked.

Miss Humm looked down her nose. 'Some of the men dress up as women in the pantomimes and musicals—if that's what you mean, Sergeant. The only serious performer is young Gerald Turner. He plays female parts sometimes. Marvellous to watch, too.' She wagged her head admiringly.

'Is that so?' Millson exchanged a look with Scobie. 'Good at playing a woman, is he?'

'So good you wouldn't know he wasn't one,' said Miss Humm.

Driving on down the hill, Scobie said, 'Easy enough to break in with those locks. That's if he didn't have keys of his own.'

'Thinking of Gerald Turner are you, Norris?'

'Well, seems he's a first-rate female impersonator and you yourself thought he was hiding something.' Scobie brought the car to a halt in front to Baxter's house.

Millson paused in opening the door. 'He said he wasn't in Tanniford on Saturday, he was visiting his mother in hospital. Have that checked, Norris.'

Millson called the detectives and support staff together in the Incident Room and briefed them as Scobie distributed copies of the blown-up video picture.

'This may well be the man who abducted the child,' Millson told them. 'He could have hidden her in the pram and that would be how he got her away unobserved. No one would have paid particular attention to him because there were a number of other men with prams and dressed like that moving about the fête. That's why it's important for you to get precise times and full descriptions of any sightings so we can discriminate between this man and the others. We have a list of these men from the organizer of the Pram Race and we'll be interviewing them first. And I want the statements we've taken looked through for any mention of men dressed as nannies.'

He swept the assembly with his eyes. 'It's essential we identify this man—and the pram.'

*

After the briefing, Millson went to see Carol Brown. She was sitting in her front room with the WPC. As soon as she saw him her eyes widened in fear.

'There's no news,' he said quickly. 'I just want you to look at a picture. It's of someone who was at the fête on Saturday . . . someone we haven't identified yet.' He showed her the blow-up of the video picture.

She looked at it. 'Someone in the Pram Race?'

'That's just it. He wasn't. He didn't take part.'

She looked at the picture again, longer.

'Could he be anyone you know?' Millson asked.

'It's impossible to say. You can't really see his face.'

'Is there anything about the way he's standing . . . his height . . . build . . . *anything* about him?'

She shook her head.

'Well, it was just a chance,' he said.

She raised swollen red eyes. 'Did he take my Maisie?'

'We don't know. But we have to find him.'

Millson returned to the Incident Room and called a press conference. He announced there had been a new development. A WPC handed out copies of the picture as he told reporters the police were anxious to trace this man dressed as a nanny at the fête on Saturday. They knew of a dozen such men who'd taken part in the Pram Race, he explained, but this man hadn't entered the race and they would very much like to talk to him.

'Presumably he could be an innocent participant in the fête?' someone suggested.

'Oh yes.' Millson faced the nearest camera. 'This man could be totally innocent and quite unconnected with the abduction. However, we need to identify him in order to eliminate him from our inquiries.'

At the coroner's court in Colchester that morning, PC Baxter gave evidence of being called to Spring Street and finding Ernie Turner's body lying on the pavement outside his house. Gerald Turner followed him into the witness-box. He testified in a firm voice that his father had left no note, but had been very upset by his mother's death and said he couldn't face life without her.

After hearing medical evidence, the coroner returned a verdict that Ernest Turner took his own life whilst in a state of acute distress following the tragic death of his wife. Closing the proceedings, the coroner expressed sympathy for Gerald on his double bereavement.

After the episode in Tanniford Woods, Charles Cresswell had begun meeting Gerald after school and taking him for drives in his car. Gerald told his mother he was rehearsing for a new play.

One evening Cresswell asked Gerald if he'd like to act in a film. 'Mr Nunn and I have set up a small studio above my office.'

'What sort of film?'

'One that suits your talents perfectly. You'll play a girl called Geraldine. That's what you like, isn't it?' Cresswell's voice was caressing. 'And we'll pay you, of course.'

The other participant was a fair-haired boy called Bobby North who took the male part. He was a year or two older than Gerald and went to the same school.

The nature of the film became apparent at the first session. There was no proper script and hardly any dialogue. Cresswell directed the scenes—sometimes joining in the action himself—and Sidney Nunn recorded them with his video camera.

After the initial shock Gerald accepted his role and played it realistically. Acting in front of a camera—being able to cry and scream, totally unconstrained—fascinated him. And it *was* acting, he told himself . . . even art of a sort.

Gerald was now a confirmed transvestite. Donning

female clothes brought him a strange comfort, a kind of relief. And his mother's acceptance of this secret behaviour freed him of guilt. He acquired a selection of wigs and hairpieces and practised his art with increasing skill. It was no longer enough for him to appear in a play or the occasional pantomimes and comedy sketches at the village hall. He wanted more. More thrills . . . more daring.

One day he took the train to Colchester, carrying a wig and some of Rachel's clothes in a small suitcase. He changed and applied his make-up in the toilet on the way. When he left the train and walked out into the street dressed as a woman for the first time, he almost fainted with excitement.

After that, masquerading in public had become a regular treat for Gerald Turner.

CHAPTER 11

The first reports that afternoon from the house-to-house inquiries were disappointing. Plenty of people had seen men dressed as nannies on Saturday around the time of the Pram Race, but the information was confused and conflicting. And the few reported sightings of the man in the picture were also confusing. One witness thought she might have seen him in West Street, another in East Street. Both put the time at five past four and neither was sure in which direction the man was heading. And when shown the newspaper photograph of the contestants, they became doubtful whether the man they'd seen was the one in the video picture or one of the contestants.

Millson threw the reports back on the collator's desk. 'Might or might not be! Don't know which way he was going!' He glared savagely at Scobie.

A WDC approached nervously. 'Sir?'

'What?'

'There's a Trudy Wilson in the waiting-room. DC Jones brought her in. She gave him a positive sighting of the man.'

'Right! Bring her to my office.'

He turned to Scobie. 'She's our page one girl, isn't she?'

'That's right. Nice legs.'

'You would notice them,' Millson said sourly.

'Couldn't help it. They were about all you could see of her.'

Today when she entered Millson's office and sat down, Trudy Willson's legs were encased in skin-tight, black leather trousers with a silver-studded belt. On top she wore a black leather waistcoat.

Unlike Gladys Humm and Ronald Craig, sitting eyeball to eyeball with Chief Inspector Millson didn't bother Trudy.

She opened her pert young face to him in a friendly smile and by a flick of her head, included Scobie in it as well.

She came straight to the point. 'That guy in the picture—I saw him on Saturday.'

'Where?'

'He come out of West Street pushing a pram as me and Wayne—Wayne's me boyfriend—was walking down to the quay. He crossed the High Street right in front of us.'

Millson snapped his fingers at Scobie. 'Map!'

Scobie produced a street map of Tanniford from his pocket and spread it in front of Trudy.

'Show me!' Millson commanded.

She bent forward, golden hair brushing Millson's face. 'Right, we comes out the churchyard here . . .' she laid a slim forefinger on the map and traced their route, '. . . walks down the High Street and as we reaches the bottom this guy comes outta West Street,' a tapered fingernail indicated the spot, 'and walks into East Street.'

'What time was this?'

''bout five past four. We'd just been called over the speakers to get down the quay for the Race.'

Millson peered at the map. 'So this man was heading in the wrong direction?'

'Well, he could've been looking for his partner—'cept he didn't turn up at the start.'

Scobie leaned forward. 'He could have continued along to Spring Street, couldn't he?' Gerald Turner's house was in Spring Street.

'Yeh, I guess so.'

'Did you get a look at his face?' Millson asked.

'Well . . . no. I was too busy clocking his outfit. Me and Wayne was after the prize for the best-dressed couple, see?'

Scobie opened his notebook. 'You can give us a good description of what he was wearing, then?'

'Oh yeh . . . sure.' Trudy closed one eye and screwed up her face. 'Wig was grey. A big bonnet—black straw . . .'

She put her hands to the sides of her head. 'Come down like this and hid his face . . .'

'It's called a poke bonnet,' Millson said.

'Yeh?' Trudy was impressed. 'Well, he had a black shoulder cape, white shirt and black skirt. His legs was bare and he had black shoes.' Her blue eyes crinkled at the corners. 'Didn't reckon he had much chance of winning in that get-up,' she said.

Scobie turned back the pages of his notebook to the descriptions Miss Humm had given them. 'This cape and skirt—could they have been blue?'

Trudy wrinkled her forehead. '*Blue?*'

'Police blue,' Scobie explained.

Her face cleared. 'Oh, like coppers wear. Yeh, that's right, they was.'

'What about his height?' Millson asked. 'Short? Tall?'

'Medium.'

'And his build? Was he fat or thin?'

'Difficult to say with that long cape he was wearing.'

'Age?'

Trudy shrugged. 'Could've been any age under his make-up.'

'And no one with him?'

'No. When he didn't show up at the start I thought his partner must've chickened out.'

'What about the pram? Anything in it?'

'The hood was up. Looked like a mattress and blankets inside.'

'And you've no idea who he was?'

She pursed her lips, thinking. 'Sorry, no.'

'Your boyfriend . . . Wayne. He saw the man too?'

'Shouldn't think so.' She giggled. 'He was having trouble seeing anything with the false eyelashes I stuck on him. Worth it, though. We won the prize.'

'Congratulations.' Millson beamed at her. 'Thank you, Trudy, you've been very helpful.'

'My pleasure,' she said.

She stood up and bobbed her head in farewell, her dangling earrings narrowly missing Millson's nose.

'Bright girl,' Millson said as the door closed behind her.

He leaned back in his chair and lit a cigarette. 'Gerald Turner's alibi had better be solid. What's the score on that, Norris?'

'They're still trying to contact the ward sister who was on duty Saturday afternoon,' Scobie said.

Millson gave a snort of impatience. 'Go and have a word with Kathy Benson. Find out what time he left her place on Saturday.'

Kathy Benson looked up with a smile when Scobie came into the estate agent's. She had taken a liking to this tall, sandy-haired policeman with the friendly face.

Scobie returned the smile. Last night's kiss lingered in his memory and he planned to kiss her again at the first opportunity.

'I'd like to ask you about Gerald Turner, Kathy. He was away on Saturday, I believe.'

'That's right. He asked for the afternoon off to visit his mother.'

'What time did he leave?'

'Two o'clock.' She frowned. 'Why?'

'Just routine.'

Her frown deepened. 'Norris, don't be an idiot. You can't suspect Gerald of being the nanny.'

'Why not?' Her scornful tone stung him into adding, 'He's a member of the Tanniford dramatic society . . . the clothes came from their wardrobe . . . he specializes in playing females—'

'You *do* think it was him!'

'Not necessarily. It's simply that we have to explore every possibility,' he said defensively.

Kathy stamped her foot. 'You're being ridiculous! I've

known Gerald since he was a child. It wasn't him who grabbed me at Alresford Creek. I'd have known.'

'I told you . . . the Chief Inspector doesn't think that incident had anything to do with the kidnap,' Scobie muttered.

'Well, *I* do!' Kathy's eyes glinted angrily. 'I believe Maisie was taken out of Tanniford by boat and—'

A car horn blared outside in the street. Millson's blue Sierra was at the kerb. At the wheel, Millson was beckoning imperatively.

'Excuse me . . .' Scobie went out to him.

'Get in!' Millson threw open the passenger door. 'I've just had a message. Gerald Turner didn't show up at the hospital until seven o'clock Saturday.'

Gerald Turner checked the knot of his black tie in the hall mirror. The inquest had gone off smoothly, with no awkward questions and a lot of sympathy. Now there were only the funerals to face tomorrow. That would be pretty awful. He'd never been to a funeral before, let alone a double one. And there'd be lots of people there—half the village probably.

A car stopped in the street outside. He looked through the window and saw Millson and Scobie get out.

'I'd like to ask you some more questions,' Millson said, when Gerald opened the door. His grim expression and tone of voice made Gerald Turner feel queasy inside.

His face was dead white against the black suit as he showed the two men into the sitting-room. They sat down, stiff and upright, on the sofa. He lowered himself into an armchair and saw the sergeant take out a notebook.

'When I spoke to you on Sunday you told me you weren't in Tanniford Saturday afternoon,' Millson said. 'You told me you were visiting your mother in hospital.' His blue eyes locked on to the boy's brown ones. 'That wasn't true, was it?'

Gerald Turner swallowed. They must have checked with the hospital. 'No, I didn't see my mother until the evening.'

'Why was that?'

'It's terrible watching someone you love slowly dying. I knew she was near the end. And I-I . . .' He caught his breath. 'I couldn't face it.'

'So what did you do?'

'I went for a walk in the park and waited until my father came.'

'Where? What park?' Millson snapped.

'The Castle Park . . . in Colchester.'

'I see.' Millson's face was expressionless. 'I gather you're pretty good at impersonating a woman?'

Scobie saw a wave of shock pass across Gerald Turner's face.

'I take a female part sometimes,' he said cautiously. 'On stage,' he added.

'*Only* on the stage?'

Turner's eyes widened. He stared at Millson like a frightened rabbit. 'Yes . . . of course . . .' His voice was strained.

Millson leaned forward, eyes boring into Gerald Turner's. 'What about last Saturday? At the fête? Dress up as a woman then, did you?'

The brown eyes were panic-stricken. Gerald had never dared to masquerade in Tanniford. Not until last Saturday, when the village was thronged with strangers. Last Saturday he'd returned to the house while his father was down on the quay and put on his prettiest dress. He'd made up carefully, then slipped out and mingled with the crowds. It had been a crazy thing to do, but he'd had to relieve the screaming tension inside him. He simply couldn't face that awful-looking skeleton in the hospital bed again without a palliative.

Pointless to try and explain to this grim-looking policeman, though. He wouldn't understand.

He sagged in his chair. 'How did you find out?' he whispered.

Millson looked surprised at the sudden collapse. Scobie stared down at his notebook, his expression deadpan. Gerald Turner had broken easily—he was about to confess to abducting Maisie. Kathy had been entirely wrong about him.

Millson opened his briefcase and took out the video picture. He pushed it at Gerald. 'That's you, isn't it?'

Gerald looked confused. He took the picture and glanced at it. 'No, that's not me.'

'What?' Millson's voice was a growl.

'That's not me, that's a man in drag.'

Millson took a deep breath. 'Let me get this straight,' he said patiently. 'You admit you were at the fête on Saturday dressed as a woman?'

'Yes.'

'But that isn't you?' Millson's finger stabbed the picture.

'No, it's some bony oaf in nursemaid's clothes. I wouldn't be seen dead looking like that.' Gerald Turner had regained his composure.

There was a long silence. Scobie stole a glance at Millson. He sat, staring down at his waistcoat, brooding.

Finally, Millson raised his head and said stubbornly, 'I don't believe you. I think it *is* you.' He leaned forward and tapped the picture in Gerald Turner's hand.

'You can *see* it isn't,' Gerald insisted. 'Where was it taken?'

'By the railway bridge as the procession was returning to the car park.'

'I was standing a bit further down, nearer the Falcon.'

Millson reached into his briefcase and took out another picture. It was the group of spectators from which the enlargement had been made. He held it out.

'One of these people, were you?' he asked sarcastically.

Gerald Turner leaned forward and studied the group. He pointed. 'Yes. There! That's me.'

Millson gazed sceptically at the dark-haired girl in a summer dress. 'Oh yeh?'

'Yes, I can prove it!'

Gerald jumped to his feet and ran lightly upstairs. He returned with a white polka-dot dress draped over his arm. Holding the dress to his shoulders, he struck a pose, hip and leg thrust provocatively forward, head thrown back. The eyes were open wide, their expression alluring. Scobie was amazed at the transformation.

Millson studied the dress. He examined the figure in the front row of the spectators again, looked up at Gerald for a while. He seemed lost for words.

At last he said, 'OK, I believe you.' His tone was grudging. 'Why didn't you come forward? You must have seen the appeals on television and in the papers.'

Gerald Turner hung his head, looking more like a girl than ever. 'I couldn't very well, could I?'

Millson glowered at him. Among the yellow pins on the Incident Room map was an unaccounted for girl outside the Falcon. A girl, described by a witness as wearing a white dress with black polka-dots. No one had followed her up because they'd been concentrating on the men. He sighed heavily. Didn't do to overlook a thing.

Scobie said, 'You were quite near the man we're interested in. Did you notice him?'

Gerald Turner dropped the dress on to a chair and drew his brows together daintily. 'Yes, vaguely. I saw him again later, pushing the pram across the High Street. He was in a hurry. He went into Station Road.'

Scobie looked up from writing. The entrance to Baker's Passage was in Station Road . . . behind Kathy Benson's place. 'You actually saw this man enter Station Road?'

'Oh, yes . . . definitely.'

'What time was this?' Millson demanded.

'Well, the church clock struck four soon after, so it must have been a minute or two to four. Is he the kidnapper, then?' Gerald asked anxiously.

Almost certainly, after what you've just told us, Millson thought. Aloud, he said, 'Possibly.'

Standing with Scobie in front of the Incident Room map, Millson rummaged in a box of map pins and picked out some little red flags. He stuck one into the corner of Station Road.

'Gerald Turner saw the man there just before four o'clock. The man enters Baker's Passage from the top end and—' he stuck a second flag into the map—'snatches Maisie at the junction with Blood Alley. He ties her up, puts her in the pram then continues along Baker's Passage and comes out at the bottom into West Street. He wheels the pram eastwards along West Street and Trudy Wilson sees him here—' he dug a third flag into the map—'at five past four.'

Millson stood back and surveyed his additions. 'He's our man, all right, Norris. And he's here in Tanniford.' He picked out a white pin from the box. 'Might as well complete the picture.' He inserted the pin into the cluster of coloured pins outside the Falcon.

The map-plotting clerk looked up from his desk. 'What's that, sir?'

'A fairy,' Millson said. 'Sergeant Scobie will explain.'

Gerald Turner took his father's letter from the drawer where he'd hidden it and tore it into tiny pieces. He dropped the pieces into a metal wastebin and set fire to them with his father's lighter. Then he took the bin out to the back garden and scattered the ashes over the flower beds.

On Sunday evening, when Ernie Turner visited his wife for the last time, he'd sat with her throughout the night. In the early hours of Monday, just before she died, Rachel told him about her and Gerald. Ernie thought she was hallucinating, her mind fogged with morphine.

By the time he returned to Tanniford, however, the

doubts had begun. He broke into Gerald's room. The evidence had been damning . . . irrefutable.

Ernie poured out his feelings of revulsion and betrayal in a letter and left it on the kitchen table. Then he mounted the stairs to the top of the house and hurled himself to his death.

The forensic examination at the scene of the fire in the church tower was undertaken by a young scientist called Croft. His examination was brief but thorough, and his conclusion—when he reported it to Millson that afternoon—was firm. The fire had been started deliberately . . . with petrol. He'd be able to say what grade when he'd examined samples in the laboratory.

'He probably laid a strip of cloth across the floor to the stairway as a delay fuse to give him time to get away,' Croft told the Chief Inspector.

'*He?*'

Millson's sharp bark made Croft jump. He'd joined the service only recently and they'd warned him about Chief Inspector George Millson. 'Chew your balls off, given half a chance,' they'd said. Mentally, David Croft placed a protective hand over his gonads.

'Chief Inspector, I admit the *possibility* of a woman,' he said politely. 'But the statistics are against it. There have been very few women arsonists.' With a smile, he added, 'And I didn't notice any lipsticks or female hairs lying around.'

'Did you look?'

Now this wretched policeman with the shaggy eyebrows was questioning his competence. Somehow, their roles had become reversed . . . the layman instructing the expert.

'No, I didn't,' he said lamely. 'But I will.'

'Yes, just in case,' Millson said mildly. 'You never know. Anything else?'

'Only that it was lucky the fire brigade were on the scene so quickly. Another minute and the roof would have caught fire.

It's a wooden roof laid in pitch and it would have burnt like fury.'

Millson scratched his neck above the collar. 'Wonder what the motive was.'

'That's your department, Chief Inspector,' Croft said crisply. 'I'll let you have my written report as soon as possible.'

'Thanks.' Millson's face relaxed in a fleeting smile.

The smile made David Croft feel better and he departed believing—quite wrongly—that George Millson's bark was worse than his bite.

Later that afternoon he phoned from the laboratory. 'Thought you might like to know it wasn't plain petrol, it was an oil-petrol mix,' he told Millson. 'The sort used in an outboard engine. Oh, and by the way . . . there were lots of hairs around, of course—male *and* female. I gather the tower roof was open to visitors during the fête.'

Millson had known that all along. He refrained from comment. He'd made his point.

The man watched the evening television news as usual. He sucked in his breath as the picture of himself in the nanny outfit appeared on the screen. It was so clear . . . so detailed.

He was agitated for a while, until he'd satisfied himself it wouldn't get them anywhere. The pram was safely hidden—in case he needed it again to move her—and he'd burnt the clothes in the stove on Saturday night. Including her red dress.

She'd made a fuss about taking it off. Her mum'd kill her if it got messed up, she said.

'That's why you have to take it off,' he told her.

'I ain't got nothing else to wear,' she said.

He gave her an old shirt.

'I can't wear that.'

'Do as you're told or I'll belt you!'

She'd taken the dress off quickly enough then.

FRIDAY

CHAPTER 12

At the funeral service on Friday morning, Kathy Benson sat with Gerald Turner. He'd looked so lost and bewildered sitting alone in the front row of the pews, she'd felt impelled to move forward and sit beside him.

He showed no emotion at the graveside when his father's coffin was lowered into the ground. But as the undertaker's men threaded the straps through the handles of his mother's coffin and removed the planks beneath it, he reached for Kathy's hand and gripped it fiercely. Tears ran down his cheeks.

Afterwards, he returned with her across the churchyard to the office. Starting work again would take his mind off the funerals, he insisted.

Charles Cresswell had also attended the service. He watched them walk away, frowning as he saw Gerald lay his head on Kathy's shoulder.

Yesterday afternoon Sidney Nunn had phoned him after Millson's car returned past his shop.

'The police have been questioning Gerald.' Nunn's voice was agitated. 'And I'm worried. Old Alice says he's been blubbing like a baby these last few days.'

'Emotional bed-wetting,' Cresswell said. 'He needs a new mum.'

'But suppose he told them about the films we made with him and Bobby North?'

'There's no reason why he should. Stop worrying. I'll go and see him. It's time I expressed my condolences anyway.'

Cresswell walked from the boatyard to the house in

Spring Street and knocked on the door. Gerald Turner opened it.

'May I come in?' Cresswell entered without waiting for an answer. 'I was very sorry to hear about your mum and dad, Gerald,' he said softly. 'If there's anything I can do to help . . . *anything* . . .' He took hold of the boy's hand.

'No! I'm all right.' Gerald jerked his hand away.

'As you wish. Sidney tells me you've had a visit from the police.' Cresswell spoke gently. 'What did they want, Gerald?'

The boy gave a petulant toss of his head. 'They were asking about Dad's suicide,' he lied. 'Wanted to know how well he'd known Maisie.' He saw Cresswell's look of relief. 'Why? What did you think it was about?'

Cresswell shrugged. 'When they questioned Sidney they took away one of his videotapes. I thought perhaps . . .' His voice tailed away.

Gerald's lip curled in a sneer. 'Afraid I'd tell them about your dirty films? Well, I didn't.'

'I'm glad to hear it.' Cresswell turned to leave. 'I meant it about helping, Gerald. You've only to ask.'

Soon after Kathy and Gerald Turner reopened the office, Charles Cresswell drew up outside in his silver BMW. He stepped in through the door, greying hair well-groomed, dark blue suit perfectly tailored. A prosperous, respectable business man.

'How's your sister, Kathy?'

'She's just about holding herself together.'

'Terrible business . . . terrible.' Cresswell glanced at Gerald Turner's red-rimmed eyes. 'So much unhappiness,' he murmured. His gaze returned to Kathy. 'I dropped in to ask you to put the house in Ferry Street on the market again.'

The house—a 'two up-two down' terrace—was known as 'The Castle' because of the castellated parapets to the front and rear of the flat roof. Cresswell had bought it cheaply a few months ago and put it up for sale again at a higher price. Kathy had been about to advertise the house for him when Cresswell withdrew it and his new manager, Frank Belmer, moved in.

'Will it be with vacant possession?' she asked.

'Yes, Belmer's moving out soon.'

'I see. Well, it might suit Trudy Wilson and Wayne Green. They're getting married in the autumn and looking for a place of their own. Can I show them over?'

Cresswell pursed his lips. 'I don't see why not. I don't suppose Belmer will mind.'

His grey eyes smiled warmly at her and moved to Gerald Turner again. The boy lowered his eyes and looked away.

As the BMW drove off Gerald muttered, 'I hate that man.'

Kathy looked at him in surprise. 'Mr Cresswell? Why?'

Gerald hesitated. He'd buried the past with that ritual handful of earth thrown on to the coffins. Except . . . the ghosts were still with him. He wanted to be rid of them. To unburden himself. Kathy was warm . . . sympathetic . . . What would she think of him, though? It would be better to reveal his involvement with Charles Cresswell in a more roundabout way—by telling her about someone else.

'He corrupts people. He corrupted Bobby North.'

Kathy said in surprise, 'You knew Bobby North?'

'Oh yes. He went to my school. And we did some acting together in a film.'

He gave Kathy a sanitized version of his and Bobby's part in Cresswell's film-making.

'I did it for the acting. Bobby did it for the money. The scenes Cresswell made us perform got more and more disgusting and in the end Bobby wouldn't do them. Cresswell was furious. He said Bobby had wasted his money—his investment he called it. Bobby didn't care—he said there were easier ways to get money. Next thing I knew, he'd been caught robbing Mrs Mullins.'

'You make him sound hard done by, Gerald.' Kathy's tone was cool. 'Bobby didn't just rob her, he beat her up. A defenceless old woman.'

A sulky expression appeared on Gerald's face. 'That was your sister said that. Bobby told me she was lying—swore he'd pay her out.'

Kathy asked sharply, 'Are you sure about that?'

'Oh yes. He was right churned up about it.'

Charles Cresswell found Frank Belmer waiting in his office when he returned. Not waiting respectfully like an employee, but lounging in his armchair. Cresswell's mouth wrinkled with displeasure. Really, the man was becoming insufferable.

He sat down at his desk. 'Did you want to see me about something?'

'Came to tell you I'll be leaving Monday.'

'Oh . . . right.' Cresswell didn't trouble to hide his gladness.

'And to let you know I'll be borrowing *Moonstreak* for a while. She's not booked out to anybody.'

Cresswell's jaw dropped. 'I beg your pardon.'

Moonstreak was Cresswell Marine's fastest cruiser and always in demand. An alarm bell began ringing in Cresswell's mind. Something was very wrong if *Moonstreak* was free at the height of the season.

He eyed Belmer cautiously. 'Do you mean you're hiring *Moonstreak* yourself?'

'No, I mean you're lending her to me—free, gratis and for nothing. I need a holiday and a place to live while I find another job. She'll do just fine.'

'Don't be ridiculous!' Cresswell's voice rose. 'It's out of the question.'

Belmer said calmly, 'Maybe you'd rather I opened my

mouth about the naughty videos you've been bringing in from Amsterdam.'

Cresswell stiffened in his chair. 'What are you talking about?'

'Now don't be stupid and play the innocent,' Belmer said nastily. 'I've only to walk up the road to the coppers and they'll be down here faster then you and Nunn can zip up your flies. I can give them dates . . . times . . . names and addresses of your customers . . . the lot.'

Cresswell stared at him aghast. 'Where'd you get that information?'

'Same place I got this. It's a sample of some photos I could send your wife . . . and a few other people.' He tossed a photograph on the desk.

Cresswell looked at it and turned pale. It was a photograph of himself and Gerald Turner, one of a set he kept in his safe. He'd taken them with a delayed action shutter.

'You bastard! You've been in my safe.'

'That's right,' Belmer said coolly. 'Careless, the way you keep the keys in your desk drawer. Now . . . do I borrow *Moonstreak* or not?'

Cresswell said through tight lips, 'Seems I don't have a choice.'

'That's settled then,' Belmer said comfortably. 'I'll be taking her out Monday morning. And think yourself lucky. You're getting off lightly. I could take you to the cleaners with what I've got.'

In the saloon bar of the Black Dog at lunch-time, Norris Scobie self-consciously sipped a beer. He was aware of a faint hostility towards him in the crowded bar. Antipathy had developed between the villagers and the police. The people of Tanniford were certain Maisie Brown's kidnapper was not one of them. George Millson was equally certain he was. He'd concentrated police effort on the villagers and they resented it.

The police were pursuing other lines of inquiry as well, of course, interviewing known sexual offenders in the area and researching previous cases of missing children. The customers in the bar of the Black Dog were unaware of these activities, however, and cast suspicious glances at Scobie quietly consuming his drink.

Earlier, he'd telephoned Kathy Benson to apologize for his abrupt departure yesterday afternoon.

'Perhaps we could meet for a drink?' he suggested.

'That would be nice.'

'The Black Dog . . . say one o'clock?'

'I'll be there,' she promised.

Carol Brown was in tears when Kathy called to see her. She was slouched on the sofa, her blonde hair lank and uncombed.

'Ronnie's left me,' she said listlessly.

And good riddance to him, Kathy thought. Aloud, she asked, 'What's made him do that?'

'He said he couldn't stand the upset and the gloom any longer. He's gone back to his wife.'

Kathy sat down beside her and took her hand. 'I'm sorry, Sis.'

'I feel so alone,' Carol said miserably. 'Maisie . . . Ronnie . . .' She clutched at Kathy. '*You* won't leave me will you, Kathy?'

'Of course I won't.'

'I know I've been rotten to you—'

'Ssh . . . don't talk about the past. We both made mistakes.'

Kathy stroked her sister's hair, memories of childhood flooding in. Carol needing her hurts made better, Kathy the healer. For a while they were quiet together.

'Carol, dear, I came to ask you about Bobby North.'

Carol wiped her eyes and sat up. 'What about him?'

'When you gave evidence at his trial . . . was it the truth?'

'Why do you ask?'

'Bobby North told Gerald Turner you lied.'

'I didn't lie.'

Wearily, Carol turned her head away. Perhaps she hadn't told the truth either, or not the exact truth. It had been near enough, though.

On a cold, moonless night last December, she'd been returning from an evening class in Colchester. Mr Cresswell had paid for a course in word-processing for her so she could operate the new equipment he'd installed in the office.

It had been after eleven when she walked along West Street from Tanniford station. As she turned the corner into Bath Street, she heard a noise in Vy Mullins's house a few doors along. The sound of someone falling downstairs.

She ran to Vy's front door. It was ajar. She pushed it open. At the foot of the stairs, a hooded figure was struggling with a prostrate Vy Mullins. Carol screamed. The attacker broke away and rushed past her into the street. He fled into West Street and collided with two men walking home from the Station Arms. Alerted by Carol's scream, the men seized him and pulled off the balaclava. Underneath was the frightened face of Bobby North.

Before the police took a statement from her the next morning, Charles Cresswell called Carol into his office.

'I've been on to the hospital and sent some flowers to Mrs Mullins,' he told Carol. 'Poor old soul.' He catalogued the injuries. 'Black eyes, a broken arm, three ribs fractured . . . A dreadful attack . . . utterly dreadful. It's a miracle she's not dead.'

He'd seen the chance to punish Bobby North for rejecting him and wrecking his film project and it was too good to miss. 'I know this boy. He's a vicious young thug. You ask Mr Nunn. This is not the first time he's done something like this . . .'

Cresswell painted her a frightening picture of Bobby

North. A picture that Carol—his loyal secretary—accepted. Then he went over with her what she'd seen in Vy Mullins's house, subtly colouring and reinterpreting the details until Carol viewed the scene differently.

'He was punching and kicking Mrs Mullins as she lay on the floor,' she told the police later that morning.

Vy Mullins's own account of what happened was confused. She remembered encountering a hooded figure on the landing and grappling with it. After that, she wasn't sure. A sensation of falling . . . sudden pain . . . then nothingness until she came to in hospital.

On the day, two months ago in May, when Carol gave evidence at the trial, Cresswell rehearsed her in what to say.

'Lay it on a bit thick,' he advised, 'or he'll merely get probation. And then he'll attack some other helpless old lady.' Cresswell hinted darkly at what more Bobby North might do next time.

At the end of the trial the judge described Bobby as a menace to society and sentenced him to three years in prison. Carol believed she'd helped put a violent young criminal out of circulation.

'I may have exaggerated a little,' Carol admitted to Kathy, 'but he deserved everything he got. He was a nasty piece of work. Mr Cresswell told me all about him.'

Kathy frowned. Charles Cresswell might have influenced her deliberately. There was no point in saying so though, or worrying her with Bobby's threat of revenge.

Kathy returned to her flat and changed from the sober grey suit she'd worn to the funeral into a summer dress of apple green. Leaving Gerald Turner in charge of the office, she walked down the High Street and along West Street to the Black Dog.

There was a lull in the conversation as she entered the

bar and joined Scobie. She knew why. The locals regarded drinking with Detective-Sergeant Scobie as consorting with the enemy. Ignoring the disapproving glances, Kathy took Norris Scobie by the arm and steered him through a door at the side of the bar into a small room on the other side of the counter.

The Black Dog was the only pub in Tanniford to retain a private bar for privileged customers. Kathy's father had often used it for business discussions with clients. She caught the barman's eye as she opened the door, daring him to challenge her. He gave her a feeble smile and nodded.

'I say, this is cosy,' Scobie said, when they were sitting alone in the room with their drinks.

'I haven't brought you in here to be cosy,' Kathy said firmly. She reached up to the hatch in the wall through which the drinks had been served and closed it. 'It's so we can talk freely. Can you check if someone is in prison for me?'

'I could, yes.' Scobie hid his disappointment. He'd drawn the wrong conclusion from Kathy's desire for privacy. 'Is this connected with Maisie?'

'It might be. It's certainly to do with Carol.' She told him of Bobby North's threat. 'He believes she lied about him in court.'

'And did she?' Scobie asked.

Kathy hesitated. 'She may have made things sound worse than they were. She says he's a villain.'

'And you think it might be him kidnapped Maisie? To get his own back? It's a bit far-fetched, Kathy. Besides, you say he's in prison.'

'That's what I'm asking you to check.'

'OK. It's no problem.'

'Thank you, Norris.' She looked at him over the rim of her glass. 'What do your friends call you?'

'Norrie.'

'Norrie?' She considered it. 'I prefer Norris.'

*

Millson was in his office when Scobie returned. There was an empty glass on the table and on a plate beside it the crusts of half-eaten sandwiches.

He gave Scobie a sour look. 'Nice lunch?' he inquired.

'Beer and sandwiches, same as you.'

'Pleasant company though?'

They usually took meals together when they were working. Scobie realized Millson resented being left on his own.

'It wasn't entirely social,' he said defensively. 'I did gather some new information.'

He told Millson about Bobby North. 'According to Gerald Turner, he made threats against Maisie's mother. I promised Kathy I'd run a check on him.'

Millson brushed crumbs from his waistcoat. 'Not sure I'd believe Gerald Turner. But you'd better do it.'

There was nothing fresh in the evening television news. He was disappointed there were no new pictures of Carol Brown. He went to a cupboard and took out some tins. Time for the kid's supper.

'Why you keeping me here?' she asked, when he took it to her.

'Never you mind. Eat your grub.'

'You're gonna kill me, aren't you? You can't let me go 'cos I know who you are.'

'No, I'm not going to kill you.'

Not yet, anyway.

SATURDAY. Morning . . .

CHAPTER 13

On Saturday morning Kathy took Trudy Wilson and Wayne Green to view 'The Castle' in Ferry Street. The narrow street of terrace houses was on the other side of the churchyard from the High Street. It had no pavements and the front doors of the houses opened straight on to the street. 'The Castle' was one of the houses that backed on to the churchyard.

Kathy hadn't made an appointment, relying on Frank Belmer being at home on a Saturday. He was, but decidedly unwelcoming when he opened the door to her knock.

'What d'you want?'

His straw-coloured hair was tousled and his shirt gaped open above his trousers revealing hair of the same colour on his abdomen.

'I'm from Benson's Estate Agency,' Kathy said.

'I know who you are,' he said rudely. 'What d'you want?'

Kathy clamped her mouth against an angry retort. 'Mr Cresswell said it would be all right to show this couple over the house.'

'He didn't tell *me* that,' Belmer said belligerently.

'Well, would it be convenient?'

'Not very. I'm just off to work. Saturday's a work day for me,' he said peevishly.

'There's no need for you to be here,' Kathy said. 'I can show them round.'

He said quickly, 'No, I'll stay.' He stood aside for them to enter.

Kathy had seen Belmer around the village a few times

since he'd started work at Cresswell Marine, but hadn't encountered him face-to-face. Close to, as she stepped past him into the house, his pale blue eyes were cold and unblinking.

The front door opened directly into the front room. Kathy opened her folder of particulars and began reading them to Trudy and Wayne.

'A through-lounge with original sash windows and tiled, Victorian grate . . . Dining alcove under the stairs . . .'

She'd typed out the particulars two months ago when the house was first up for sale. As she enumerated the features she cast a professional eye about her to see if they were still correct. The house was grubbier than when she'd seen it before. Clearly, Belmer didn't bother with housework.

'Is the furniture being left?' Trudy asked, looking askance at the faded upholstery and sagging curtains.

The elderly couple who'd lived there previously had been moved into an old people's home by their son. Cresswell had bought the house as it was, complete with furniture.

'No. The furniture will be cleared out and the place thoroughly cleaned before handing over,' Kathy assured her.

They moved on into the kitchen. The sink was full of dirty crockery and on the table there were half-empty cans of soup and baked beans.

Belmer followed as Kathy led the couple upstairs. The bed was unmade in the front bedroom and in the bathroom there was a tidemark of dirt round the bath. From a clothes rack propped across the bath hung a row of socks. Belmer suddenly pushed forward and gathered them up.

'I'd have tidied up if you'd let me know you were coming,' he said.

The back bedroom overlooked the churchyard. One corner of the room was filled by a double-fronted Victorian wardrobe tight up against the low ceiling.

Wayne looked upwards. 'How d'you get into the loft?'

'You can't. There isn't one,' Belmer said.

'It's a flat roof,' Kathy explained. 'The original roof was destroyed by fire about twenty years ago and the people who owned it then couldn't afford a pitched roof.'

Returning downstairs, she concluded there was no change to the particulars of the property. Everything was the same as when she'd viewed it before. Except outside.

Stepping through the kitchen door into the yard, Kathy read aloud from the sheet in her hand: 'West-facing paved patio . . . with small garden—' She looked up and stopped.

She turned to Frank Belmer. 'There was a garden shed here, wasn't there?'

He seemed thrown by the question. After a moment he said, 'I got rid of it. It was rotten . . . like the rest of the old tat in this place.'

Kathy took a pen from her handbag and amended the particulars. She wondered if Charles Cresswell knew the shed had been removed.

In the Incident Room, Norris Scobie picked up the phone and rang Chelmsford prison.

Yesterday afternoon, using the terminal link to the Police National Computer, he'd confirmed Robert North's conviction and three-year sentence in Criminal Records. He'd had to wait until this morning for the Home Office Prison Index at Bootle to tell him in which prison North was serving sentence.

He asked the admin office at Chelmsford to confirm North was still being held. A few moments later he heard his call being transferred to the Governor.

'North topped himself a month ago,' the Governor told him. 'Hanged himself from the gallery rails with a bedsheet.'

'Any idea why?'

'Mental stress, according to the coroner. That's the current euphemism.'

'Meaning?'

The Governor sighed. 'A nice-looking boy of eighteen banged up with the scum we've got in here? Do I really need to spell it out for you, Sergeant?'

Frank Belmer's expression changed to a mocking sneer as he closed the door on Kathy Benson and her clients. He'd nearly refused to let them in and he'd have been justified, since she hadn't made an appointment. It might have seemed suspicious though and as he was always prepared for an unexpected call by the police, there had been nothing lying about to arouse comment. Except that pair of white socks. He was sure no one had noticed them before he scooped them up.

It had been a shock when she asked about the shed. It hadn't occurred to him it might be mentioned in the particulars of the property. Ten days ago he'd taken it apart and carried the sections upstairs to the rear bedroom. He'd dragged the empty wardrobe aside. In the ceiling above it a rectangular trapdoor gave access to the flat roof.

He'd discovered the trapdoor by accident soon after he moved in. It was obvious it hadn't been used for years. The hinges were rusty and so was the sliding ladder above. Later, when he was making his plan, the trapdoor had given him the idea of where to hide her while the hunt was on.

He'd manœuvred the sections of shed up on to the roof and re-erected them against the side wall of next-door's loft. The shed was out of sight there from the ground or the upstairs windows of neighbouring houses.

He nailed struts across the window, fitted a padlock to the door and installed a camp bed and chemical toilet borrowed from the boatyard. He covered the shed with the translucent plastic sheeting used to cocoon the motor-cruisers during the winter. Finally, he carried out tests with a radio inside the shed at full volume to satisfy himself shouts and screams wouldn't reach the street or nearby houses.

This morning, with people standing in the room right beneath the shed, he'd worried they'd hear something. He'd been ready to create a diversion, but there had been no sound from above.

He decided to take her up a bar of chocolate for a treat before he left for work. As though she deserved a reward. A reward for not being able to make herself heard. She was certain to have been thumping and screaming. Sometimes he listened outside the shed when she didn't know he was there. For the last two days she'd shouted and banged regular as clockwork, every half hour.

'Help! I'm Maisie Brown. Help me!'

'That's the end of that line of inquiry,' Scobie said when he reported Bobby North's suicide to Millson.

Millson scratched his chin. 'Not necessarily.'

'How d'you mean?'

'North committed suicide because of what happened to him in prison, right?'

'Right.'

'And he wouldn't have gone to prison if it hadn't been for Carol Brown's evidence, right?'

'Right.'

'So doesn't it occur to you, Norris, that someone might blame *her* for his suicide? Be very angry about it? Especially if they knew she fabricated her evidence.'

Scobie's brows came together. 'I hadn't thought of that.'

'Then think of it now. Ring the prison. Find out who was his next of kin . . . who claimed the body . . . and go and see them.'

Millson spent the rest of the morning reviewing the information and studying statements. Everyone in the vicinity of Blood Alley at four o'clock on Saturday had been accounted for. Except the man dressed as a nanny. The whereabouts of every man in the village at that time had been verified and plotted on the map. Which meant the man with the pram—if he lived in Tanniford—and Millson was convinced he did—had to be someone who was thought *not* to be in Tanniford on Saturday.

Methodically, Millson went through the list of men who'd said they were elsewhere, matching them with the reports of the follow-up inquiries. Every absence had been checked and found to be correct—except Gerald Turner's, of course.

He lit a cigarette and scrutinized the names again. One other man living on his own who'd said he wasn't in Tanniford on Saturday, was Frank Belmer. Belmer said he'd been in Brightlingsea from Friday evening to Sunday morning. Millson re-read the report of the DC who had checked the story.

According to the barman at the yacht club, Belmer was in the bar at closing time Friday night. He saw him working on a Cresswell Marine cruiser on the moorings Saturday afternoon and served him in the bar again Saturday evening. Several club members confirmed seeing Belmer there.

Millson puffed at his cigarette, recalling his interview with Belmer last Sunday. He hadn't liked the man. Though that meant nothing, of course. According to his ex-wife he didn't like anyone. 'The trouble with you, George, is you don't like *people*. You think everyone's a villain.'

Although they hadn't asked, Belmer had insisted on taking him and Scobie round the house—opening cupboards and showing them the backyard. He gave exact times and a string of witnesses for his time in Brightlingsea. People weren't usually able to supply information like that so readily and Millson suspected he'd rehearsed his story beforehand.

George Millson had an ability to detect emotions by

smell. Belmer, he remembered, smelt of anger. Suppressed anger. What was the man so angry about? He gnawed his lip. He had doubts about Frank Belmer. He decided to interview him again.

At midday Belmer returned to the house for his lunch and to check on his captive and feed her. Soon after, there was a knock on the door. Opening it, he masked his alarm at finding Chief Inspector Millson on the doorstep. Belmer's eyes flicked up and down the street. Millson was alone. He relaxed.

'I'd like to go over your movements on Saturday again if I may, Mr Belmer.'

'Yes, sure. Come in.'

Millson took a seat with his back to the window, so that Belmer was facing the light.

'Tell me again what you were doing in Brightlingsea from Friday to Sunday, Mr Belmer.'

'Certainly. The moorings here dry out at low tide and our hire cruisers sometimes have to use the moorings at Brightlingsea downriver. That's what happened last Friday.'

Belmer explained that the cruiser *Leonie*, returning from a week's hire, had berthed at Brightlingsea Friday evening. He'd gone downriver to meet her on another cruiser, *Emerald*, which was due to be picked up from there Sunday morning. He'd stayed on *Leonie* Friday and Saturday night and brought her back on the tide Sunday morning after he'd handed over *Emerald*.

'Several people saw me in Brightlingsea,' Belmer said confidently. 'The family who returned *Leonie* . . . people in the yacht club bar Friday . . . the harbourmaster—I spoke to him a couple of times on Saturday and—'

'Did you know Maisie Brown?' Millson interrupted abruptly and watched Belmer's eyes.

'No.' They were steady, not a flicker.

'Her mother?'

'No.' Again no reaction.

'Have you lived in Tanniford long?'

'No, only a month or so. Since I took the job at Cresswell Marine.'

'And before then?'

'I've worked abroad for the last ten years. The last place was a marina in Gibraltar.'

'D'you own a car, Mr Belmer?'

'No. Can't afford one.'

Belmer was sure they would already have checked with DVLC Swansea. And probably worn down their shoe leather tramping round car hire firms to see if he'd hired one.

'Are you married?'

'Divorced . . . ten years ago.'

'And you're on your own here?'

That was a laugh. 'Yes, all alone.' Must watch he didn't giggle.

'Made any friends in Tanniford?'

Careful. This was dangerous ground. Neighbours might notice he never left the house in the evenings.

'No chance of that. Up to our elbows at the yard this time of year. I'm shagged out by evening. Besides . . . I'm leaving Monday.' He noted the slight rise of Millson's eyebrows and went on with deliberate casualness, 'I told Cresswell I'd be leaving a couple of weeks back.'

That had been a vital element in the plan. To announce his departure *before* he snatched her so no one would attach any significance to his leaving.

Millson stared moodily in front of him. Belmer had answered the questions glibly, as though enjoying himself. Millson was familiar with the syndrome. Over-confidence . . . quick answers . . . a sense of superiority. A man who was convinced he was impregnable. Millson decided to re-investigate this smart alec's story for himself.

He said mildly, 'Thank you, Mr Belmer, that seems to clear up everything.'

'Only too glad to help.'

A flash of triumph in the pale blue eyes. Millson read excitement too. Belmer was hyped on his own cleverness.

Closing the door on the Chief Inspector, Frank Belmer let out a giggle. He was giggling a lot lately. They were fools . . . the police . . . Cresswell . . . the whole village.

He could hardly wait to get up there and look at her again. When she was frightened she looked like her mother. He enjoyed that. Like the moment he'd taken her out of the sailbag. The terrified face. So much like that bitch, Carol, he'd nearly spoiled his plan and killed her there and then.

Soon, he'd be away from here and no one the wiser. With the kid on board *Moonstreak* on some lonely mooring, he'd carry out the second phase of his plan.

He must keep control, though, or he'd make a mistake. He took some deep breaths. When he was calm he locked the front and back doors and went upstairs.

Moving the wardrobe aside, he opened the trapdoor and went up on the roof. He unfastened the padlock and opened the shed door.

SATURDAY. Afternoon . . .

CHAPTER 14

Norris Scobie returned along the A12 from Ipswich feeling depressed. A phone call to Chelmsford prison that morning had produced the information that Bobby North's next-of-kin was his father and he lived in Ipswich with Bobby's mother.

'Neither of them came to see him,' the chief officer told Scobie. 'He only had the one visitor. A man about forty. Came several times.'

Scobie had driven to Ipswich to see Mr and Mrs North. They were a drab, tired-looking couple living in a rundown block of council flats. They told him Bobby had left home a year ago when they moved from Colchester.

'We moved to Ipswich because of my husband's job,' said Mrs North. 'Bobby wouldn't come with us. Walked out on us. That's the thanks we got for bringing him up like our own.'

'Adopted, see,' Mr North explained. 'Bad blood. Not surprised he came to a nasty end.'

Scobie felt sorry for Bobby North. He must have had a rotten childhood with this miserable pair.

'There was a man who visited him in prison,' he said. 'Any idea who he was?'

They shook their heads.

'Did he mention anyone in his letters, perhaps?'

Mrs North's mouth set in a hard line. 'He never wrote. And we didn't go to see him.'

'We didn't have anything to do with him after we left Colchester,' said her husband. 'Why are you asking these questions?'

'Just routine. We're trying to trace someone.'

Mrs North sniffed. 'Could have been his friend, I suppose.'

'Who was that?'

'An older man,' she said, her mouth drooping. 'It started when he was at school.'

'Can you describe him?'

'Middle-aged . . . grey hair. Looked like a business man.'

'He had plenty of money, I believe,' said Mr North. 'Bobby let slip he owned a boatyard. Didn't give his name, though.'

Scobie knew who he was. Charles Cresswell. Could Cresswell have been outraged by the boy's suicide and taken revenge on Carol Brown? As chairman of the Dramatic Society he probably had access to the costume wardrobe. He couldn't have been the nanny, though, because he'd been umpiring the Pram Race.

Driving back to Tanniford to see Cresswell, Scobie had a wild thought. What if the nanny hadn't been a man dressed up, but a woman? A woman acting for Cresswell. A woman pretending to be a man pretending to be a woman. He shook his head. Gerald Turner's description had been: 'A man in drag.' And he should know.

Kathy thought Trudy and Wayne had been put off 'The Castle' by its slovenly state and Belmer's unpleasant manner. They'd departed saying they wanted to think it over. To her delight, however, in the middle of the afternoon Wayne phoned to say they'd decided to buy.

When Kathy phoned Charles Cresswell to tell him the news she asked if the garden shed had been included in the sale price.

'Not really, because it was new last autumn,' he said. 'But since they haven't haggled over the price, I'll throw it in.'

Kathy put down the phone. *The shed was almost new*. Why

had Frank Belmer lied? And why had he been so shocked when she asked about it? There had been something else too. The house was in a state . . . dirty dishes, bed not made, grime round the bath . . . Belmer hadn't cared or apologized. Until they came to the washing in the bathroom. He'd whipped those socks away quickly, as though they mattered in all the chaos. She'd seen the flashes of white, though. White socks . . . *small* white socks. A child's socks?

'Who shall I say it is?' Zena Baz asked Scobie. In Carol Brown's continued absence, she had graduated to being Charles Cresswell's temporary secretary.

'Detective-Sergeant Scobie.'

Zena's large blue eyes grew larger. She announced Scobie on the intercom phone and showed him in.

'What can I do for you, Sergeant?' Cresswell asked heartily, rising from his chair.

'I believe you knew Bobby North,' Scobie said bluntly.

Cresswell sank back into his chair. 'Yes.'

'Did you visit him in prison?'

'Certainly not!'

'But you were on familiar terms with him, I understand.'

Cresswell suddenly looked worried. 'I tried to help the boy . . . I felt sorry for him. That's all.' His tone was defensive. 'Why? What's he done now?'

Scobie raised his eyebrows. 'You didn't know he committed suicide?'

'No!' Cresswell's surprise was genuine. 'I'm sorry to hear that.' He looked relieved too.

'I'm trying to trace anyone who might have been close to him. His parents mentioned you. Do you know of anyone else?'

'Well, there's his mother—his *real* mother, I mean. Bobby was adopted.'

'Yes, I know.'

'She contacted him some time last year.'

'Do you know where she lives?' Scobie asked.

'He didn't tell me her actual address. She lives in Suffolk . . . Monks Eleigh. Shouldn't be difficult to find her. She calls herself Stigall—Mrs Stigall.'

'Thanks.' Scobie turned to leave.

'Do they know why he killed himself?'

'Too much of the same thing you had going with him, I believe,' Scobie said grimly.

Driving away from Cresswell Marine, Scobie stopped at the estate agent's and called in to see Kathy Benson. She was at her desk, busily typing.

'I dropped in to let you know about Bobby North.' He told her of the suicide.

'I'm afraid I wasted your time then.'

'Not at all. He could have been a lead.' He glanced at the pile of finished letters on her desk. 'Busy?'

She sighed. 'Just paperwork. I sold a house today.'

'Congratulations. Whereabouts?'

'In Ferry Street. A man called Belmer lives there and . . .' She hesitated for a moment then decided to share her anxiety with Scobie. '. . . there's something odd there.'

She told him about the missing shed.

To her annoyance Scobie laughed. 'He probably sold it and pocketed the money.'

'You don't know that,' she said crossly. 'Suppose he didn't and he's moved it somewhere? There have been cases of kidnapped children kept in sheds near their homes, haven't there?'

He said patiently, 'Kathy, we've searched every square inch of this village and the fields for miles around. There isn't a shed anywhere we haven't looked in, I promise you.'

'Well, there's something else. I saw some socks in the bathroom . . . white, like Maisie was wearing.'

'They were his, I expect. Men do wear them, you know.'

'You needn't be so dismissive,' she said sharply.

'I didn't mean to be. Look, Kathy, Belmer wasn't even *in* Tanniford on Saturday. We checked.'

'I don't care. There's something not right in that house. I could feel it. But I can see it's no use expecting you to understand. I'm sorry, I thought you would.'

He looked at her unhappily. He had another reason for calling in, although now didn't seem a good moment to ask. 'Can I see you tonight?'

'Perhaps,' she said coolly, 'if I'm not busy.'

'I'll stop by at eight o'clock.'

She nodded.

Soon after Scobie's car drove out of the gates Cresswell emerged from his office and told Zena, 'See you Monday. I'll be at home if I'm needed.'

He descended the outside staircase to the quay where *Moonstreak* was lying. Frank Belmer was swabbing the deck.

'I take it you'll still be here Monday morning?' Cresswell said coldly.

Belmer nodded. 'I'll want me wages before I leave.'

Cresswell considered demanding Belmer's assurance he would bring the cruiser back at the end of the fortnight. What would be the use? Of course he'd say yes.

His mouth set. 'See you Monday then.'

Belmer touched his cap in mock salute. He watched Cresswell drive off in his BMW with a sardonic grin. That was him out of the way. Belmer had no intention of waiting until Monday. He was leaving tomorrow night on the tide.

Frank Belmer had come to Tanniford soon after Bobby North's suicide. He had one thing in mind. To make Carol Brown suffer.

He'd listened to her from the public gallery in Colchester Crown Court a month before, spouting her lies about Bobby, sewing him up neatly, like a body in its shroud. It wasn't true what she said, Bobby swore to him it wasn't.

Frank Belmer was Bobby North's brother. Or rather, his half-brother. Until six months ago Frank had no idea he had a young brother. He'd lived abroad, working as a barman or waterman and returning occasionally to visit his mother. Frank didn't know who his father was. Neither did his mother. He could have been any one of several men.

Last December Frank Belmer had received an urgent summons to return home. His mother was dying.

At her bedside in the cottage in Suffolk, he encountered a stranger. A youth with blonde wavy hair and light blue eyes.

'This is your brother,' his mother told him. 'His name's Bobby. Bobby North. I had him adopted when he was a baby, but I kept track of him. When I knew my time was come I sent for him.' Her wasted hand came from beneath the bedclothes and took hold of his wrist. 'He's in trouble with the law. Promise me you'll look after him, Frank.'

He looked across the bed at his new half-brother. Bobby's deep blue eyes gazed back at him, full red lips parting in a warm smile. Frank Belmer experienced an unusual emotion. He patted his mother's hand.

'I promise, Ma.'

After their mother died, Frank and Bobby lived on at the cottage. Frank, who'd had a failed marriage and some unsatisfactory affairs, discovered a new kind of relationship with Bobby. And Bobby found the father figure he'd always sought. The two of them bonded together like glue. December to May, while Bobby was on bail awaiting trial, was a time of happiness for them.

Frank was sure Bobby would be given probation when the case came to court. He believed that right up until he sat in the public gallery listening to Carol Brown in the witness-box.

Bobby told him he'd tried to escape when Vy Mullins caught him on the landing of her house. She grabbed hold of him though and in the struggle they fell down the stairs together.

'I didn't hit her, Frank. Not once. The old biddy was out cold, hanging on to me—hands tight closed like she was dead. I was trying to make her let go . . . when this Carol bird come in the door.'

Frank listened as defence counsel put it to Carol that what she'd seen was Bobby entangled with Mrs Mullins and trying to free himself. 'Tugging . . . not punching,' he suggested.

'No,' Carol insisted, 'he was punching her. He hit her again and again. It was terrible.'

The more counsel tried to shake her, the more details she added. Charles Cresswell had convinced her she must strengthen her story, otherwise the odious Bobby North would get off.

Defence counsel tried to persuade the jury Mrs Mullins's injuries were caused by her accidental fall down the stairs. The prosecution had already scotched that idea though.

'Accident?' Prosecuting counsel was derisive. 'This was no accident! This frail old lady was *thrown* down the stairs. Then—lying there helpless—she was viciously attacked.'

The jury found Bobby guilty. Guilty of attempted robbery. Guilty of causing grievous bodily harm.

'After hearing the evidence of Mrs Carol Brown,' the judge told Bobby, 'I am satisfied you beat this elderly lady mercilessly. You are a menace to society. You will go to prison for three years.'

Three years. Frank Belmer was devastated. Three years for a first offence. It was diabolical. That lying bitch! She was the one responsible for having Bobby banged up. Not the prosecution. Not the judge. Not the jury. *Her*. Carol Brown.

After the trial Frank told Bobby, 'Hang in there, boy. You'll get remission and time'll soon pass.'

But eighteen-year-old Bobby North, with blonde wavy

d rosy cheeks, hadn't been able to stand what the prisoners did to him. At visiting times, Frank listened in horror as Bobby told him. Listened and burned inside.

Bobby's spirit had soon broken. When Frank Belmer heard he'd hanged himself he went berserk. In the cottage in Monks Eleigh he smashed up the furniture and howled like an animal in pain. When his mind cleared he was obsessed with one purpose. To take revenge on Carol Brown.

He couldn't believe his luck when Cresswell offered him a job and a place to live in Tanniford and he found Carol Brown was Cresswell's secretary. The first time he encountered her face-to-face he nearly lost control. He wanted to reach out, take her neck in his hands and choke her to death.

He set about planning his revenge. What would hurt her most would be to lose her daughter. She loved Maisie. As he'd loved Bobby. He'd make Carol suffer the way he'd suffered . . . and find out what it was like to lose someone you loved.

He would kidnap Maisie. When he was satisfied Carol had suffered enough, he'd release the child. Maybe.

Millson turned off the Brightlingsea road and down Tenpenny Hill on his way back to Tanniford feeling frustrated. He'd hoped to uncover a flaw in Belmer's story. A reason for forensic to scour the house for a hair, a fibre . . . anything to link the man with Maisie Brown. All his visit to Brightlingsea had done was to confirm Belmer's story. Belmer had undoubtedly been in the yacht club Friday and Saturday night. And the barman said he'd seen him aboard *Leonie* on Saturday afternoon.

'He called me up on her ship-to-shore phone,' the barman said, 'and asked what was for lunch. I told him fish and he said he wouldn't bother.' The barman pointed through the club window to a row of moorings. 'He was out there. *Leonie* was moored on the first buoy, with *Emerald* alongside. Her hatch was open . . . ensign and house flag flying . . . dinghy lying astern. No question he was on board.'

Once he'd set up the makeshift prison on the roof, Belmer was ready for the kidnap. Maisie went to Brownies on Wednesdays and dancing classes in the village hall on Fridays. And she always walked home along Blood Alley. That was where the snatch would take place, he decided.

There was the problem of getting her from the alleyway to the house without being seen though. It seemed insurmountable—until posters announcing the fête appeared in the village. Maisie was performing with the majorettes. And there was a Pram Race. Men dressed as nannies . . . wheeling prams. The perfect disguise, the ideal means of transport . . . and the village crowded with strangers.

He would steal an outfit from the village hall and he knew where to lay his hands on a pram. Clearing the outhouse at his mother's cottage ready for the sale, he'd come across an ancient four-wheeler. Rusty, but still serviceable. He'd pick it up in the van one night.

Belmer's office at Cresswell Marine was adjacent to Carol Brown's, separated by a thin hardboard partition. A few days before the fête there was a rehearsal by the majorettes and Maisie called in to see her mother afterwards.

Through the partition he heard Carol say, 'On Saturday you go straight home when the parade finishes and change out of your uniform. Straight home. Do you hear?'

And the child answering, 'Yeh, yeh. OK.'

He knew then the plan would work.

Kathy paused in typing a letter to Cresswell's solicitor, confirming the sale of 'The Castle'. A scene returned to her . . . the rear bedroom . . . explaining the flat roof to Wayne. Belmer had been listening, but his attention had been elsewhere. People's eyes tended to look in the direction of what they were thinking about. Belmer's had turned upwards.

Suddenly, a door in her mind opened on a monstrous thought. It was totally absurd, of course, she told herself. She'd inspected the house when Cresswell first put it up for sale and she'd seen over it again today. There was no access to the roof—not even a skylight.

The idea persisted though, nagging, preventing her resuming her work. She abandoned the half-finished letter and went to a filing cabinet in the room behind the office. It contained her father's old records of properties bought and sold over the years. She searched through them until she found the particulars of the house in Ferry Street at the time of an earlier sale—after the roof had been rebuilt.

Her eyes raked the page. 'Back bedroom . . . sash window overlooking churchyard . . . *trapdoor in ceiling giving access to flat roof* . . .'

Kathy sagged against the cabinet. Why hadn't she seen it? Had it been covered in? Or was it hidden by that huge wardrobe? If it still existed . . . if he hadn't sold the shed and . . .

'Oh, my God!' She began to shake.

She ran upstairs to her flat and looked out of the window at 'The Castle' on the other side of the churchyard. It wasn't possible to see the roof because of the castellations along the parapet.

She stemmed her tumbling thoughts. The police must have visited the house—they'd visited every house in the village. Had they known about the flat roof, though? Norris Scobie would tell her. She lifted the phone . . . then replaced it. He'd just think she was fantasizing again, he wouldn't take her seriously.

She stood biting her lip. It was crazy to think Belmer had kidnapped Maisie and was keeping her prisoner in a shed on the roof. Utterly crazy.

She knew she wouldn't rest until she'd looked, though.

She glanced at her watch. Belmer would be at work—he'd said today was an ordinary workday. It wouldn't take a moment to reassure herself, rid herself of this crazy fear.

She hurried downstairs to the office and picked up the keys from her desk.

'I'm just going out for a while,' she told Gerald Turner. 'Shan't be long.'

Frank Belmer turned off the water hose, replaced the deck cap and recoiled the hose. He'd filled the water and fuel tanks to capacity. Now it only remained to put aboard the food he'd stored in the house. He jumped down from the deck of the cruiser and climbed into the driving seat of the Cresswell Marine van.

Cresswell had caved in easily over *Moonstreak* as he'd known he would. Bobby had once told him Cresswell imported pornographic videos from Holland. It hadn't taken him long, snooping around after hours in the office, to find the evidence. Addresses of customers . . . stock lists of videos . . . letters to Van Beck in Amsterdam.

Kathy let herself into 'The Castle' and stood inside the front door, listening. Although, as Cresswell's agent she had a right to enter the house and a good excuse if she was challenged, she felt frightened.

She called out, 'Hallo? Anyone home?'

The house was silent. With an impatient toss of her head at her cowardice she made for the stairs.

The ceiling in the back bedroom was smooth and unbroken, no sign of a boarded-up trapdoor. She looked doubtfully at the heavy wardrobe, its top touching the ceiling. Tentatively, she grasped a corner and heaved. To her surprise the wardrobe moved and she realized it was empty. Exerting her full strength she pulled it away from the wall. Panting, she looked up. There, in the ceiling, was the trapdoor!

On the floor where the wardrobe had stood was a slim pole with a hook on the end. Kathy picked it up and hooked the catch on the trapdoor. The trap swung down on its hinges revealing a folding ladder. She hooked the end of the ladder with the pole and pulled. The aluminium ladder tilted and slid smoothly down, its two sections unfolding.

Kathy dropped the pole and climbed the ladder.

Belmer got out of the van and went down the side passage to the kitchen door. He went in and lifted a carton of tins from the table. He turned, then stopped, frowning at the faint aroma of perfume. There was a sound above him. He dropped the carton on the table and leapt to the stairs, padding swiftly up them.

Kathy Benson clambered out on to the flat roof and saw the amorphous outline under plastic sheeting against the wall of the next house. She bent and lifted a corner, catching her breath at sight of the shed. Hauling the sheeting aside she rapped on the padlocked door.

'Maisie?'

An arm was thrown round her neck from behind, choking her. A knife in the other hand rose level with her mouth.

'Keep quiet or I'll cut your throat!' Belmer snarled.

SATURDAY. Evening . . .

CHAPTER 15

Norris Scobie drove away from the Suffolk village of Monks Eleigh at seven o'clock. He'd spent the day chasing back and forth across the county and he was tired and hungry. Earlier, he'd found a shopkeeper in the village who'd known Mary Stigall.

'She died last Christmas,' he informed Scobie.

Mary Stigall had lived alone for years, he said, but shortly before her death a young boy and an older man came to live in the cottage. They continued living there after she died, so he supposed they were related to her. They left in May and then the cottage was sold.

Scobie asked if the youth's name was Bobby North. 'I think he was called Bobby, yes. Nice-looking boy . . . fair hair . . . blue eyes.'

'And the older man?'

'Supposed to be his brother.' The shopkeeper snorted. 'More like lovers than brothers they were, if you ask me.'

Scobie's interest sharpened. 'Could you describe him?'

'Didn't see much of him. Late thirties, I'd guess . . . well-built . . .'

Scobie wondered if he was the man who'd visited Bobby in Chelmsford prison. 'You say he was affectionate towards Bobby?'

'Doted on him, I'd say.'

Scobie called on the new owners of the cottage. It stood on its own on the edge of the village. The cottage was empty when they viewed it, they told him, and the sale was handled by solicitors acting for the executors. They knew nothing of the previous occupants.

Scobie tried the nearest neighbours. They too had no information about the two who'd shared the cottage. 'Kept themselves to themselves,' they said.

Driving back to Tanniford, Scobie decided he'd contact the solicitors who sold the cottage and see if they could put a name to the man living with Bobby North. That would have to wait until Monday, though, when they were open.

Kathy Benson sat on a chair in the back bedroom of 'The Castle' gazing fearfully at Frank Belmer as he stood over her with a long-bladed sheath-knife. Above them was the rectangle of sky in the ceiling and the ladder down which he'd forced her at knifepoint.

She'd been a fool. She should have waited, or at least left a message for Norris Scobie. Now she was at the mercy of this monster who'd kidnapped Maisie . . . and who'd attacked her last Saturday night. His arm round her neck a moment ago—choking off her scream—was an arm in a blue pullover . . . the same blue as the thread of wool lying in her office drawer.

He was glaring at her balefully. She fought down her panic, desperate to know if Maisie was alive.

'Maisie's up there in the shed, isn't she? Is she . . . all right?'

'She's OK.' His eyes slewed away from hers and she wondered if he was telling the truth. 'What made you come back?'

'The shed . . . Mr Cresswell said it was new. That . . . and the socks in the bathroom. Then I found out about the trapdoor and—'

'And you had to come and poke your nose in,' he said viciously, hefting the knife in his hand.

She must be brave, remain calm . . . for Maisie's sake.

'My office knows I'm here,' she said firmly. 'And if you don't let us go—'

'Shut up! On your feet.'

He pulled her from the chair and pushed her out of the room and down the stairs.

Downstairs, he picked up the telephone. 'What's the number?'

With a sinking feeling, she told him. He rang the estate agency. Putting on a falsetto voice, he asked for Miss Benson.

'She's not here at the moment,' Gerald Turner said.

'When will she be back?'

'I can't say, I'm afraid. She went out and didn't say where she was going.'

Belmer replaced the phone. 'You lying bitch.' He smiled unpleasantly at Kathy.

He wasn't going to let her spoil his beautiful plan. He'd take her with him, that's what he'd do. Out at sea, he'd wind her round and round with anchor chain like a mummy and put her over the side. She'd lie on the bottom till Kingdom Come. Or, better still, he'd keep her for a while. There was room enough on *Moonstreak* to keep two prisoners battened down below. She could do the cooking and washing.

He wouldn't wait until tomorrow now, he'd leave as soon as possible. Couldn't leave in daylight, though. And the tide was dropping. By the time it was dark there mightn't be enough depth of water at the quay for *Moonstreak* to get out.

Belmer looked at his watch. He had time to load the stores aboard and put the cruiser on to to a deepwater mooring, where she'd lie afloat for hours yet. He'd have to ferry his captives out to the cruiser by dinghy, but that would be safe enough in the dark. He made up his mind.

Picking up the phone again he thrust it at Kathy. 'Now you're going to tell some more lies,' he said, pointing the knife at her throat.

*

In the estate agent's Gerald Turner answered the phone again. It was Kathy Benson.

'Something's come up, Gerald,' she said. 'A property deal. It's hush-hush and I'll be away for a few days. I'm sure you can cope.'

'When will you be back?'

There was a pause. Then, 'I don't know,' she said. 'Don't worry, I'll phone you again.'

Belmer took a coil of nylon rope from a cupboard under the stairs and pushed Kathy upstairs again and into the front bedroom. He uncoiled the rope.

'Hands behind your back,' he ordered.

'Don't tie me up . . . *please.*'

'Do as you're told or I'll cut your face!'

Swiftly and expertly, he bound her wrists. Pushing her face down on the bed, he lashed her ankles together then hauled them up behind and tied them to her wrists. He turned her over and, ignoring her pleas, taped her mouth with parcel tape.

His eyes roamed over her as she lay on her back, trussed and helpless, her skirt rucked up to her waist. Kathy went rigid with terror. With a smirk he turned and left the room.

For a while she heard him moving about below. Then she heard the front door close and the sound of the van driving away.

Zena Baz was working late in her office on the first floor of Cresswell Marine. This was her first job and she wanted to give a good impression, so she'd stayed behind clearing up after Charles Cresswell went home.

She glanced out of the window. Down on the quay Frank Belmer was transferring boxes from the van to *Moonstreak*. She watched him finish loading, then go aboard and start the engines. He slipped the moorings and nosed *Moonstreak* out into the river. Water creamed under her stern as the engines went full ahead and the cruiser surged across the river to a mooring downstream.

Later, after Belmer had returned in the dinghy and driven away in the van, Zena rang Cresswell at his home.

'Mr Cresswell, I thought you ought to know. After you left this afternoon Mr Belmer refuelled *Moonstreak* with diesel. Now he's loaded stores and put her out on a mooring downriver.'

'Where is he now?'

'Back in the house, I think.'

'Thank you, my dear. You were quite right to let me know.' Cresswell hung up, his face darkening with rage.

Belmer had lied. He wouldn't be here on Monday. He was leaving tonight—on the ebb tide. Otherwise he'd have left *Moonstreak* alongside the quay. Belmer intended to steal *Moonstreak*. *That* was the real price of his silence. A ninety-thousand pound cruiser! Cresswell grated his teeth. Not bloody likely!

He lifted the phone and rang Sidney Nunn. Briefly, he told him of Belmer's blackmail.

'You're in this just as much as me, Sidney. If he opens his mouth it means prison for both of us.'

At the other end of the line Nunn said angrily, 'If you give in to the sod we'll have him on our backs forever.'

'Exactly, Sidney. He has to be dealt with.'

Towards eight o'clock the activity in the Incident Room was being scaled down at the end of another day.

George Millson's office was a haze of smoke. He lit another cigarette, promising himself it would be the last before leaving for home. Home? How much longer was he going to go on hoping Dena would come and live with him? She hadn't phoned again. That meant her mother was raising obstacles about even a few days' holiday. Surely Jean wouldn't begrudge him that? He considered making a direct appeal to his ex-wife. No. He would never plead with Jean, not even for Dena.

The door opened. He looked up in surprise as Scobie came in.

'Where have you been all day?'

'Following up on Bobby North's next of kin like you told me.'

'And?'

'Well, his adoptive parents didn't care tuppence for him—and his natural mother died last Christmas. However, there was a man living with Bobby North before he went inside . . . supposed to be his brother. Worshipped Bobby apparently. No one had a name for him, but he could be the same guy who visited him in prison.'

Millson scratched his ear. 'When did North commit suicide?'

Scobie took out his notebook and flipped the pages. 'Seventeenth of May.'

'Frank Belmer came to Tanniford about then.'

'I can't see the connection,' Scobie said.

'Neither can I, but I'm not happy about Mr Belmer. I've been checking his alibi.' Millson recounted his visit to Brightlingsea. 'You're a keen yachtsman, Norris. Tell me what I'm missing. Belmer spoke to all these people on Saturday afternoon . . . the barman at the yacht club . . . the boatyard . . . the harbourmaster . . .'

'Only on the ship-to-shore telephone,' Scobie pointed out.

'Yes, but the barman *saw* him . . . out on the mooring.'

'Maybe he only *thought* he saw him. Look . . . Belmer calls him up on the cruiser's radiophone . . . and he sees the boat out there, hatch open, ensign flying. Of course he believes Belmer's there. You would, wouldn't you?'

Millson's eyes gleamed hopefully. 'Go on.'

'He could have been speaking from here in Tanniford.

The equipment is transportable and from upstairs in the house it would have the range.'

'How did he get from Brightlingsea to Tanniford? He doesn't have a car, he didn't hire one and neither of the Cresswell Marine cruisers left the harbour until Sunday morning.'

'He'd use something inconspicuous—an inflatable with an outboard . . . late Friday night after he left the bar. He lands below the village, say, hides the inflatable and walks to the house. Then he keeps out of sight until he kidnaps Maisie in the afternoon and returns to Brightlingsea in the inflatable Saturday night—taking Maisie with him.'

Millson smoked furiously for a while. He stubbed his cigarette and gave a heavy sigh. 'Full marks for theories, Norris. But that's all they are . . . theories. Not a shred of evidence to support them.'

'There might be,' Scobie said. 'And it is a shred—literally.'

'Let's have it then.'

'Well, I know you don't reckon the attack on Kathy Benson Saturday night was anything to do with Maisie's kidnap, but suppose the man was Belmer—on his way back to Brightlingsea? Remember . . . she said she heard an outboard engine.'

'You're supposing again, Norris. There's nothing to say the man was Belmer. Where's this literal shred of evidence you spoke about?'

'Kathy kept a piece of thread she tore from the man's pullover. She showed it to me. If it matches a pullover of Belmer's . . .'

Millson had risen from his chair. He opened the door and put his head out. 'Get Miss Benson on the phone,' he snapped at a WPC.

'I hope she's kept it,' he said as he sat down again. 'If nothing else, it'll give us a reason to pull him in for questioning. Just our luck she'll be out, though.'

'No, she'll be there,' Scobie said confidently. 'We have a date.'

There was a tap on the door and the WPC entered. 'Miss Benson has gone away on business, sir.'

'What? Who says?' Scobie demanded.

'The clerk, Gerald Turner. There was no answer from the estate agent's so I rang him at home. Miss Benson told him she'd be away for a while—something to do with a confidential property deal, she said. He doesn't know where.'

Scobie felt let down. Kathy had said, 'If I'm not busy,' but the date had been definite. As far as he was concerned at any rate. He thought she should have had the decency to leave a message if she couldn't make it. It depressed him that she hadn't bothered.

'She's stood you up, Norris,' Millson said. 'Your charm's not as potent as you thought.' He saw the gloom on Scobie's face. 'C'mon, I'll buy you a beer on the way home.'

'I'd rather have something to eat,' Scobie said ungraciously. 'I haven't eaten lately.'

He'd expected to take Kathy for a meal, or maybe have her cook for him again in her flat. And to follow, he'd had in mind a romantic stroll along the river bank in the moonlight.

'All right, I'll buy you supper as well,' Millson promised.

Kathy heard the sound of the van's engine again. It stopped outside the house and a moment later she heard his footsteps on the stairs. His head came round the bedroom door, eyes raking her again . . . making her flesh crawl.

'Bin a good girl, I see.'

The head withdrew and she heard the rattle of the folding ladder next door. He was going up on the roof to Maisie.

A while later she heard some heavy thumps. Craning her neck for a view of the landing, she saw him humping a section of wood panelling down the stairs. He was bringing the shed down from the roof, presumably reassembling it in the yard. Had he finished with it? Kathy shut her mind against the thought he no longer needed it because Maisie was dead.

The noises went on for a while and then the house fell quiet. Through the bedroom window Kathy saw the sky slowly darken as twilight approached. She thought of Norris Scobie. What would he think when Gerald told him she'd gone away on business? She wished now she hadn't been offhand with him, had been more enthusiastic about their date. As it was, he'd probably think she was in a huff with him because he hadn't taken her seriously about Belmer.

CHAPTER 16

The Flag Inn near Essex University was comfortably empty with the students on vacation. Millson ordered steak and chips for Scobie, nothing for himself. Mrs Baxter had sent a tray out to him earlier in the evening, he explained. 'Soup, risotto and ice-cream,' he told Scobie. 'Very nice.'

Scobie sipped a light ale and hoped the steak and chips wouldn't be long. He was starving.

'The Vicar's been nagging about that fire in the church tower,' Millson said. 'Wants to know if we've made any progress. Have we?'

'Not yet. Everyone's busy with the kidnap.' Scobie looked up hopefully as a waitress approached. She served a customer at the next table.

'Better put someone on it,' Millson said. 'Show willing.'

'OK. Funny, something like that happening when the place is alive with policemen.'

Millson flicked ash from his waistcoat. 'Perhaps it had to.'

'You mean there's a connection? Between the kidnap and the fire?' Scobie's eyes followed the waitress as she returned through the door to the kitchen.

Watching him, Millson said with a sigh, 'No I don't, Norris, I just thought it might take your mind off food if I gave you something to think about.'

Scobie turned back, 'Sorry, George. I haven't eaten all day and the hunger pangs are terrible.'

'So think about something else and they'll go away,' Millson suggested helpfully.

'OK, what?'

'For instance, why might a kidnapper set fire to the tower?'

'To stop anyone going up there, I suppose,' Scobie said.

Millson lifted his glass and took a mouthful of beer. 'Why should he care?'

'Because . . .' Scobie tried to concentrate as the door from the kitchen opened again and the waitress emerged carrying a plate of food. 'Because . . . from up there on the roof . . .'

He stopped as Millson suddenly banged down his glass. 'You can see over the whole village! That's it, Norris,' he said urgently. 'You can see something he doesn't want us to see!'

He jumped to his feet. 'Come on! Let's find out what it is.'

Scobie saw his plate of steak and chips approaching. Millson saw it too. He pulled out his wallet and tossed a ten pound note on the table. His iron fingers clamped Scobie's arm.

'No time for that now, Norris.'

Frank Belmer made a final check of the house. The shed was replaced and he'd put the camp bed and chemical toilet in the van to take back to the boatyard. The pram could be taken out to the cruiser and dumped overboard at sea. There wasn't room for it in the dinghy with two passengers. He'd have to return for it after he'd put them aboard *Moonstreak* and locked them in.

Kathy Benson had been a complication, but his plan was still intact and he'd take *Moonstreak* to an isolated anchorage up the coast and carry out the rest of it. Carol Brown was going to learn who had her daughter and why. She'd go crazy thinking about what he was doing to the kid. Before he let her know where Maisie was, he'd take the Harwich ferry to the Hook of Holland and disappear.

There was no way of tracing him. 'Belmer' was just one of several names he'd used over the years and the only two people who knew anything about him—his mother and Bobby—were dead.

Suddenly, in the quiet of the house, he giggled. Perhaps he'd change the plan a little. Make it even more satisfying. He could do anything . . . absolutely anything. No one could stop him. He looked out of the window. It was dark now, time to leave. He giggled again, louder.

In the bedroom Kathy heard the giggle and her nerves went taut. She heard him come upstairs and enter the rear bedroom. There was a dragging sound that sickened her. She wriggled to the side of the bed and strained her neck to see round the bedroom door. Belmer was dragging a heavy bundle from the rear bedroom on to the landing. He stopped and lifted it into his arms to carry down the stairs. Something bulky inside a large black sailbag . . .

Moments later he came upstairs again and into the bedroom. He bent over her and examined the tape across her mouth. Then he reached down and untied her ankles. Kathy's eyes widened in fear as he turned her on her back and stood looking down at her.

His mouth opened in another bizarre giggle. Not high-pitched like a girl's. Low . . . an animal-like gurgling in the throat. His fingers gripped the sheath-knife in the holster on his belt. Kathy's teeth clamped together in terror. She looked up into the cold blue eyes . . . vacant . . . staring . . . and knew Frank Belmer was insane.

He took a deep breath. Then another. 'You're going for a little sea trip. I'm going to put some colour in your cheeks.' He stifled another giggle.

Leaning down, he pulled her to her feet. Her legs were numb and she stumbled against him, nauseated by the contact. He took hold of her arm and led her down the stairs and out through the kitchen door.

Belmer had parked the van close against the house with the rear doors open to mask the side entrance. As he forced her along the passage, Kathy saw the waiting van and tried to pull back. Belmer seized her round the waist and bundled her in.

The doors closed and Kathy sensed, rather than felt, the black sailbag lying next to her. Maisie. Her body. He was taking it out to sea to dispose of.

Grimly, Kathy wriggled herself close against the bundle and dug an elbow into it, sharply. The bag jerked violently and Kathy's eyes filled with tears of relief. Maisie was alive!

Her relief faded. What was Belmer going to do with them? 'I'm going to put some colour in your cheeks.' Kathy shuddered and tried not to dwell on what he meant.

The driver's door slammed and the engine started.

The Reverend Vernon Smollett paused, a forkful of food half way to his mouth as Millson burst in on him in his dining-room.

'The key to the tower please, Vicar,' Millson said.

Vernon Smollett looked at him in amazement. 'Now?'

'Yes, now, please.'

'Oh, very well.'

Reluctantly, the Vicar put down his fork and went out into the hall. Opening a drawer of the hallstand, he took out a large iron key and handed it to Millson.

'Thank you. Tell me, Mr Smollett, when was the last time anyone was on the roof of the tower?'

'Wednesday afternoon. The gardener went up there to clear the leaves.'

Millson nodded. The fire had been Wednesday night. He made for the door.

'You'll bring the key back, won't you?' the Vicar called. Millson was already out of the house and heading across the churchyard.

Scobie's car drew up at the gates, a ladder strapped to the roofrack. He'd turned off into Baxter's drive as he followed Millson's Ford Sierra down the hill into Tanniford.

'Baxter's bound to have a ladder,' Millson said as they

left the Flag. 'Bring it to the tower. I'll get the key from the Vicar.'

Scobie took a torch and binoculars from the glove compartment. Unstrapping the ladders, he lifted them down and carried them across the churchyard to where Millson was unlocking the door to the tower. Millson glanced at the binocular case hanging from Scobie's neck. 'Night glasses,' Scobie informed him.

They carried the aluminium ladders up the stone stairway to the charred landing at the top. Stepping gingerly across the floor joists, they extended the ladder up to the trapdoor and set the feet on an undamaged section of the floor. The treads creaked under George Millson's weight as he mounted the ladder and pushed open the trapdoor.

Millson heaved himself out on to the roof and looked around. The cupola, for which St Mary's was famous, occupied the centre of the roof. The tower was square, the parapet castellated. Millson peered down between the castellations. The churchyard below seemed a long way away.

Scobie appeared at his side. 'Magnificent view,' he commented, surveying the scene.

'We haven't come up here to admire the view,' Millson said. 'Let's have the glasses.'

He put the night glasses to his eyes and focused them on the Incident Room trailer in Baxter's drive. Turning slowly anti-clockwise, he swept Tanniford with the glasses. The station . . . High Street . . . the houses in Bath Street . . . He lowered the glasses with a grunt of disappointment.

'What are we looking for?' Scobie asked, scanning the dark rooftops.

'I don't know till I see it, do I?' Millson snapped ill-temperedly.

He crossed to the south side of the tower and raised the glasses again, moving along the houses in Ferry Street.

'Didn't know there was a house with a flat roof,' he muttered, adjusting the focus.

He gave a hiss of surprise and passed the binoculars to Scobie. 'Take a look at the house with the flat roof . . . on the roof itself.'

Scobie put the glasses to his eyes and studied the shapeless object covered with a sheet of polythene. He could see part of what looked like a bicycle wheel protruding. But what was lying on its side beneath the sheet was bulkier than a bike.

'It's a pram! It's a bloody pram!'

'That's Belmer's house,' Millson said.

Scobie felt a sudden emptiness like the onset of seasickness. Kathy . . . leaving her office unexpectedly . . . Belmer's missing shed . . .

'He burned down the staircase when he realized you could see on to his roof from up here. Though why he didn't just hide the pram—'

'Not the pram, George,' Scobie said excitedly. 'It was the shed he was worried about! Maisie's been here all the time—right here in our midst. I should have listened to Kathy Benson when she told me about Belmer's missing shed.'

'What missing shed?' Millson asked. 'It's there in the garden. I can see it.'

'Yes, but it's been up on the roof. That's where he kept Maisie. Now he's put it back!'

'Oh hell,' Millson groaned. 'What's the bastard done with her? Come on!'

They descended the ladder and ran down the stone stairs and across the churchyard to the alleyway into Ferry Street.

Millson pounded the door of Belmer's house with the flat of his hand. 'Police! Open up!'

In the next house a man put his head out of a window. 'He's gone down the boatyard in the van,' he said.

The two policemen turned and raced down Ferry Street into East Street.

Frank Belmer drove in through the gates of Cresswell Marine and parked the van near the edge of the quay. He went to a switchbox on the wall and flicked a switch. A section of the quay, where *Moonstreak*'s dinghy bobbed at its painter, was illuminated by a small pool of light.

Returning to the van, he opened the rear doors and lifted our the sailbag. He carried it to the edge of the quay and laid it down. He went back to the van and reached inside for Kathy. Pulling her out, he prodded her towards the dinghy.

Scobie reached the yard gates first. He saw Belmer pushing Kathy in front of him, her hands tied, mouth taped. He kept control of his anger.

'Belmer!' he shouted. 'This is the police! Stop right there!'

Belmer whirled round and whipped the sheath-knife from his holster. Throwing an arm round Kathy, he pulled her against him and held the knife to her neck.

'Stay where you are, copper, or I'll cut her throat!'

Scobie froze. Behind him, Millson's running footsteps stopped.

'Keep him talking, Norris,' Millson said quietly.

Scobie's tongue was stuck to the roof of his mouth. He swallowed and studied the yard in front of him. It was empty except for the van on the quay and two cruisers to his left, propped up on baulks of timber.

He called out in a firm voice, 'The yard's surrounded, Belmer. Don't make things worse for yourself. Put the knife away and—'

'Quit gabbing, copper! There's no one else here. You're alone. You stay put. Then no one gets hurt.'

From the corner of his eye, Scobie saw Millson edge

round the gate, out of view from Belmer and move forward behind the nearest cruiser.

'Where's the child, Belmer?' Scobie called.

Belmer ignored the question. If he could keep the policeman at bay while he put his two captives in the dinghy and started the outboard, he'd be out to the cruiser and away in minutes. *Moonstreak* was capable of thirty knots. He'd be lost in the darkness before they could give chase.

He began dragging Kathy backwards. 'I'm going to put the woman in the dinghy and then the kid. You move from there and they get the knife. Understand?'

'I understand,' Scobie said quietly.

Kathy was signalling desperately with her eyes. He followed their direction and saw the bulky sailbag lying at the water's edge. His shoulders suddenly felt heavy as though a heavy weight had been laid across them. Two hostages in the hands of a maniac with a knife. A situation outside his experience. Millson had disappeared from view and he had no idea what he intended.

A few feet away from Belmer, Millson was crouching behind the bow of the second boat. Belmer was facing away from him, watching Scobie and holding Kathy in front of him as he backed towards the dinghy.

Scobie saw Millson's head emerge from behind the cruiser. His nerves, already like bowstrings, stretched tighter. Suppose he or George misjudged? He killed the thought and concentrated on distracting Belmer at the right moment . . . the moment he turned to put Kathy down into the dinghy.

Moving backwards, Belmer came level with the dinghy. He glanced down at it, turned Kathy towards it and lowered the knife. Scobie saw Millson begin to move and called out loudly.

'*Belmer!*'

Belmer turned towards him, raising his head.

'What?' The knife was pointing away from Kathy.

Millson pounced. He seized Belmer's wrist, threw his other arm round Belmer's neck and jerked the knife-hand against his upraised knee. The knife clattered to the ground.

Belmer, more powerful than Millson had reckoned with, plucked the arm from round his neck and broke free. He leapt at Kathy and thrust her into the water.

Scobie, moving fast towards him, changed direction. With hands tied behind and her mouth taped, Kathy would drown in seconds. He reached the edge of the quay and plunged in after her.

Belmer ran to the sailbag and whirled round as Millson came after him. Putting a foot under the bag, he hefted it into the water.

'She's alive!' he snarled at Millson.

Millson, not much of a swimmer, flung himself into the water and floundered towards the bag that was being kept afloat for the moment by the air trapped inside.

On the quay, Belmer ran back to the dinghy and jumped in. He started the outboard and roared off into the darkness.

Scobie reached Kathy's bobbing white face. She was frantically treading water, trying to keep her head above the surface. He ripped the tape from her mouth. She spluttered and gasped, swallowing water. Supporting her head in his hands, he towed her to the quay and pushed her unceremoniously up over the concrete edge.

He hauled himself out, snatched up Belmer's knife and sliced through the cord binding Kathy's hands.

'Where's Maisie?' she gasped as he helped her to her feet.

He stepped to the edge of the quay and peered into the darkness. There was no movement in the water. He heard choking sounds below him and looked down. George Millson, half submerged, was floating on his back supporting the sailbag on his chest. He was swallowing a lot of water.

Scobie lay down and reached out. Kathy knelt beside him and together they hauled Millson and his burden from the water. Millson rolled over on to his knees and began tearing at the cord securing the neck of the sailbag. Scobie knelt and cut it with the knife. There was no movement inside. Millson yanked the bag open muttering, 'Bastard, bastard.' He pulled the neck down over a golden head . . . a white face . . . closed eyes.

Suddenly the eyes flicked open like a doll's. They were blue eyes . . . and they were alive. Millson uttered a strangled snort and hugged the child to him, kissing her cheeks.

'Gerraway! Who you smooching?' she demanded.

SATURDAY. Night . . .

CHAPTER 17

In the glow of *Moonstreak*'s control console, Frank Belmer set the autopilot and released the wheel. He stepped down from the helmsman's seat and turned to watch the line of silvery wake gleaming in the darkness astern. Satisfied the vessel was steady on course, he opened the door to the saloon to go below for a drink.

He was safe now. He'd scuttle the cruiser by Wadgate Ledge and slip ashore at Felixstowe in the dinghy. A short walk to the Hook of Holland ferry and he'd be in Rotterdam for breakfast.

He put a foot on the top step to descend into the saloon and stopped. Someone was down there, waiting in the darkness. He stepped back quietly and reached for the boathook on the cabin roof.

'Drop that or I'll blow your head off!' Charles Cresswell stepped up into the cockpit pointing a flare pistol.

Belmer dropped the boathook on the deck. 'Listen, I—'

'Thought you'd got away with stealing my cruiser, didn't you?'

'No, I was—'

'Shut up and turn around!' Cresswell said savagely, waving the flare pistol. 'Hands by your sides.'

Belmer faced the other way, calculating his chances. Cresswell would have to lay the pistol down to tie him up . . .

Behind him, Sidney Nunn emerged from the saloon carrying a grey polythene dustbin.

'Listen, Cresswell,' Belmer began, 'I'll make a deal. If—'

His words were shut off as the bin descended over his head. Nunn rammed it down over his shoulders—pinning his arms—and on down to his knees. Cresswell kicked his feet from under him and helped Nunn turn the bin right way up. Belmer was upside down and helpless inside it, legs sawing the air.

Nunn dropped beside the dustbin, holding it steady to prevent it tipping over. Cresswell went to the control console and shut down the engines. The cruiser drifted to a stop.

He opened a locker in the cockpit and replaced the pistol in its clip, then lifted out a bucket with a rope attached. Leaning over the side, he dunked the bucket in the sea and brought it up full. He turned and poured the water into the dustbin.

Belmer panicked as the water streamed down the side and rose under his head . . . over his forehead . . . reached his eyebrows. They were going to drown him and throw him overboard. He'd be washed up on Felixstowe Beach on the next tide. The post-mortem would be straightforward—lungs full of sea water, no marks of violence on his body. The assumption would be he'd fallen overboard. He began shouting—making promises, his words muffled inside the bin.

Cresswell leaned over the side again and brought up another pailful and poured it in. Belmer's legs began cycling wildly as the water rose over his nose . . . his mouth . . .

After a while the legs stopped cycling, jack-knifed at the knees and became still. Cresswell put down the bucket and glanced at his watch.

The two men waited in silence as *Moonstreak* rocked gently to the swell of the sea.

Cresswell looked at his watch again. 'That's it,' he said.

They toppled the bin on to its side, the water flowing out and into the cockpit drainholes. Pulling Belmer's body from the bin, they carried it to the side and threw it into the sea.

Cresswell stepped to the controls and started the engines. He swung the wheel, watching the compass and steered a course for the Sunk. Staring into the darkness, he checked their position by the flashing lights of distant buoys and after a mile or so, cut the engines.

Nunn took a marlin spike from a cockpit locker, punched holes in the polythene dustbin and tossed it over the side. He climbed over the stern into the dinghy and started the outboard.

Cresswell set the autopilot and opened the cruiser's throttles slightly, enough for steerage way. He joined Nunn in the dinghy and cast off. *Moonstreak* purred away seaward, navigation lights gleaming.

Long before the Sunk, she would hit Cork Sand and be wrecked. The records at Cresswell Marine would show the cruiser as on hire to Frank Belmer and Charles Cresswell would have no difficulty recovering her cost on insurance.

He took hold of the dinghy tiller and pointed to a light winking in the distance. 'That's the Rolling Ground buoy ahead. We'll be home indoors before daylight.'

Nunn nodded and settled back in the bow seat, hunching his sailing jacket round his shoulders.

Twenty minutes later he sat upright. Above the roar of the outboard he could hear a steady thumping sound. He looked astern over Cresswell's shoulder.

'Christ! There's a ship bearing down on us!'

Cresswell glanced behind him and swore. A huge dark shape was blotting out the starlit sky. He yanked the tiller over and gunned the engine.

The men high up on the bridge of the container ship watched their radar screens, smoking and chatting, as the vessel ran over the dinghy. The dinghy and its occupants bobbed up under the stern of the ship where the churning propellers threshed them into debris. The flotsam floated for a while in the long trail of the ship's wash and then sank.

*

Early Sunday morning, Frank Belmer's body drifted in on the tide. He'd been wrong about the location, though. It was Dovercourt, not Felixstowe.

At breakfast-time, a taxi drew up outside George Millson's house. His daughter emerged with her suitcases. She hadn't come for the holidays, she informed him. She rather thought she'd stay for good, if he didn't mind.

And in Tanniford that morning, the Vicar had the church bells rung to celebrate the safe return of Maisie Brown.